BY JACK FINNEY

NOVELS

Time and Again
Good Neighbor Sam
Assault on a Queen
The House of Numbers
Fire Against the House

SHORT-STORY COLLECTIONS

I Love Galesburg in the Springtime
The Third Level
About Time
Three by Finney

NONFICTION

Forgotten News

INVASION
OF THE BODY
SNATCHERS

JACK FINNEY

SCRIBNER PAPERBACK FICTION
PUBLISHED BY SIMON & SCHUSTER

SCRIBNER PAPERBACK FICTION
Simon & Schuster Inc.
Rockefeller Center
1230 Avenue of the Americas
New York, NY 10020

First Scribner Paperback Fiction edition 1998
Published by arrangement with the author
DESIGNED BY DIANE HOBBING, SNAP-HAUS GRAPHICS

Manufactured in the United States of America

9   10   8

The Library of Congress has cataloged the Fireside edition as follows:
Finney, Jack.
Invasion of the body snatchers / Jack Finney.
p.   cm.
I. Title.
PS3556.I52I58   1989
813'.54—dc20   89-34072
CIP
ISBN 0-684-85258-6

A shorter version of this work originally appeared in *Collier's* magazine in 1954
and an expanded edition was first published by Dial in 1955 under the title
The Body Snatchers. This is a revised and updated edition.

INVASION

OF THE BODY

SNATCHERS

CHAPTER
ONE

I warn you that what you're starting to read is full of loose ends and unanswered questions. It will not be neatly tied up at the end, everything resolved and satisfactorily explained. Not by me it won't, anyway. Because I can't say I really know exactly what happened, or why, or just how it began, how it ended, or if it has ended; and I've been right in the thick of it. Now if you don't like that kind of story, I'm sorry, and you'd better not read it. All I can do is tell what I know.

For me it began around six o'clock, a Thursday evening, October 28, 1976, when I let my last patient —a sprained thumb—out the side door of my office, with the feeling the day wasn't over for me. And I wished I weren't a doctor, because with me that kind of hunch is often right. I've gone on a vacation certain I'd be back in a day or so; as I was, for a measles epidemic. I've gone to bed staggering-tired, knowing I'd be up in a couple of hours driving to a house call; as I did, have done often, and will again. I still make house calls, and so do plenty of others.

Now, at my desk, I added a note to my patient's case record, then I took the medicinal brandy, went to the washroom, and mixed a drink, something I almost never did. But I did that night, and standing at the window behind my desk, staring down at Throckmorton Street, I sipped it. I'd had an emergency appendectomy and no lunch that afternoon, and felt irritable. I still wasn't used to being at loose ends, and I wished I had some fun to look forward to that evening, for a change.

So when I heard the light rapping on the outer locked door of my reception room, I just wanted to stand there motionless till whoever it was went away. In any other business you could do that, but not in mine. My nurse had gone—she'd probably raced the last patient to the stairway, winning handily—and now, for a moment or so, one foot on a chair, I just sipped my drink, looking down at the street and pretending, as the gentle rapping began again, that I wasn't going to answer it. It wasn't dark yet, and wouldn't be for some time, but it wasn't full daylight any more, either. The street lights had come on, and Throckmorton Street below was empty—at six, around here, nearly everyone is eating—and I felt lonely and depressed.

Then the rapping sounded again, and I set my drink down, walked out, unlocked the door, and opened it. I guess I blinked a couple of times, my mouth open foolishly, because Becky Driscoll was standing there.

"Hello, Miles." She smiled, pleased at the surprise and pleasure in my face.

"Becky," I murmured, stepping aside to let her in, "it's good to see you. Come on in!" I grinned suddenly, and Becky walked in past me, and on through the reception room toward my office. "What is this," I said, closing the door, "a professional call?" I was so relieved and pleased that I got excited and exuberant. "We have a special on appendectomies this week," I called happily; "better stock up," and she turned to smile. Her figure, I saw, following along after her, was still marvelous. Becky has a fine, beautifully fleshed skeleton; too wide in the hips, I've heard women say, but I never heard a man say it.

"No"—Becky stopped at my desk, and turned to answer my question—"this isn't a professional call exactly."

I picked up my glass, raising it to the light. "I drink all day, as everyone knows. On operating days especially. And every patient has to have one with me —how about it?"

The glass nearly slipped through my fingers, because Becky sobbed, a dry, down-in-the-throat gasp, her breath sucking in convulsively. Her eyes brimmed with sudden bright tears, and she turned quickly away, shoulders hunching, hands rising toward her face. "I could use one"—she could hardly speak.

After a second I said, "Sit down," speaking very gently, and Becky dropped into the leather chair before my desk. I went to the washroom, mixed her a drink, taking my time about it, came back, and set it on the glass-topped desk before her.

Then I walked around the desk and sat down facing her, leaning back in my swivel chair, and when Becky glanced up, I just nodded at her glass, gently urging her to drink, and I took a swallow from mine, smiling at her over the rim, giving her a few moments to get hold of herself. For the first time I really saw her face again. I saw it was the same nice face, the bones prominent and well-shaped under the skin; the same kind and intelligent eyes, the rims a little red just now; the same full, good-looking mouth. Her hair was different; it was shorter, or something; but it was the same rich brown, almost black, thick and wiry, and looking naturally wavy, though I remembered it wasn't. She'd changed, of course; she wasn't eighteen now, but well into her twenties, and looked it, no more and no less. But she was also still the same woman—girl—I'd known in high school; I'd taken her out a few times in my senior year. "It's good to see you again, Becky," I said, saluting her with my glass and smiling. Then I took a sip, lowering my eyes. I wanted to get her talking on something else, before she got down to whatever the trouble was.

"Good to see you, Miles." Becky took a deep breath and sat back in her chair, glass in hand; she knew what I was doing, and went along with it. "Remember when you called for me once? We were going to a party somewhere, and you had that writing on your forehead."

I remembered, but raised my brows questioningly.

"You had *M.B. loves B.D.* printed on your forehead in red ink or lipstick or something. Said you were going to wear it all evening. I had to get tough before you'd wipe it off."

I grinned. "Yeah, I remember." Then I remembered something else. "Becky, I heard about your divorce, of course; and I'm sorry."

She nodded. "Thanks, Miles. And I've heard about yours; I'm sorry, too."

I shrugged. "Guess we're lodge brothers now."

"Yes." She got down to business. "Miles, I've come about Wilma." Wilma was her cousin.

"What's the trouble?"

"I don't know." Becky stared at her glass for a moment, then looked up at me again. "She has a—" She hesitated; people hate to give names to these things. "Well, I guess you'd call it a delusion. You know her uncle—Uncle Ira?"

"Yeah."

"Miles, she's got herself thinking that he *isn't* her uncle."

"How do you mean?" I took a sip from my glass. "That they aren't really related?"

"No, no." She shook her head impatiently. "I mean she thinks he's"—one shoulder lifted in a puzzled shrug—"an impostor, or something. Someone who only *looks* like Ira."

I stared at Becky. I wasn't getting this; Wilma was raised by her aunt and uncle. "Well, can't she tell?"

"No. She says he looks exactly like Uncle Ira, talks just like him, acts just like him—everything. She just knows it isn't Ira, that's all. Miles, I'm worried sick!" The tears sprang to her eyes again.

"Work on that drink," I murmured, nodding at her glass, and I took a big swallow of mine, and sat back in my chair, staring at the ceiling, thinking about this. Wilma had her problems, but she was tough-minded and bright; about thirty-five years old. She was red-cheeked, short, and plump, with no looks at all; she never married, which is too bad. I'm certain she'd have liked to, and I think she'd have made a fine wife and mother, but that's how it goes. She ran the local rental library and greeting-card shop, and did a good job of it. She made a living out of it, anyway, which isn't so easy in a small town. Wilma hadn't turned sour or bitter; she had a shrewd, humorously cynical turn of mind; she knew what was what, and didn't fool herself. I couldn't see Wilma letting mental troubles get to her, but still, you never know. I looked back at Becky. "What do you want me to do?"

"Come out there tonight, Miles." She leaned forward across the desk, pleading. "Right now, if you possibly can, before it gets dark. I want you to look at Uncle Ira, talk to him; you've known him for years."

I had my glass raised halfway to my mouth, but I set it back down on the desk, staring at Becky. "What do you mean? What're you talking about, Becky? Don't *you* think he's Ira?"

She flushed. "Of course; of course I do!" Suddenly she was biting her lips, shaking her head helplessly from side to side. "Oh, I don't know, Miles, I don't *know. Certainly* he's Uncle Ira. Of *course* he is, but . . . it's just that Wilma's so *positive!*" She actually wrung her hands, a thing you read about but rarely see. "Miles, I don't know what's going *on* out there!"

I stood up and came around the desk to stand beside her chair. "Well, let's go see," I said gently. "Take it easy, Becky," and I put a hand on her shoulder comfortingly. Her shoulder, under the thin dress, felt firm and round and warm, and I took my hand off. "Whatever's happening, there's a cause, and we'll find it and fix it. Come on."

I turned, opened the wall closet beside my desk to get my jacket, and felt like a fool. Because my jacket was hanging where I always keep it, around Fred's shoulders. Fred is a nicely polished, completely articulated skeleton, and I keep it in my closet, together with a smaller, female skeleton; can't have them standing around the office frightening the customers. My father gave them to me one Christmas, my first semester in medical school. They're a fine useful thing for a medical student to have, of course, but I think my father's real reason for giving them to me was because he could —and did—present them in a huge, six-foot-long, tissue-wrapped box, tied with red and green ribbon. Where he got a box that big, I don't know. Now, Fred and his companion are in my office closet, and of course I always hang my jacket on his polished bony shoulders. My nurse thinks it's a riot, and it got a little smile now from Becky.

I shrugged, grabbed my coat, and closed the door. "Sometimes I think I clown around too much; pretty soon people won't trust me to prescribe aspirin for a head cold." I dialed telephone-answering, told them where I was going, and we left the office to go take a look at Uncle Ira.

Just to get the record straight: my full name is Miles Boise Bennell, I'm twenty-eight years old, and I've been practicing medicine in Mill Valley, California, for just over a year. Before that I interned, and before that, Stanford Medical College. I was born and raised in Mill Valley, and my father was a doctor here before me, and a good one, so I haven't had too much trouble snaring customers.

I'm five feet eleven inches tall, weigh one-sixty-five, have blue eyes, and black, kind of wavy hair, pretty thick, though already there's the faintest beginning of a bald spot on the crown; it runs in the family. I don't worry about it; nothing you can do about it, anyway, though you'd think the doctors would find something. I play tennis whenever I can, so I'm always pretty tanned. Five months earlier I'd been divorced, and now I lived alone in a big old-fashioned frame house, with plenty of big trees and lots of lawn space around it. It was my parents' house before they died, and now it's mine. That's about all. I drive a 1973 Mercedes two-seater, a nice fire-engine-red job, bought used, to maintain the popular illusion that all doctors are rich.

We drove over to Strawberry, an unincorporated suburban area just outside the city limits, and then over to Ricardo Road. It's a wide winding street, and we found Uncle Ira out on the lawn in front of his house. He looked up as we slowed at the curb, and grinned. "Evening, Becky. Hi, Miles," he called.

We answered, waving, and got out of the car. Becky went on up the walk to the house, speaking pleasantly to Uncle Ira as she passed. I strolled across the lawn toward him, casually, hands in pockets, just passing the time of day. "Evening, Mr. Lentz."

"How's business, Miles? Kill many today?" He grinned as though this were a brand-new joke.

"Bagged the limit." I smiled, stopping beside him. This was the usual routine between us, whenever we ran into each other around town, and now I stood, looking him in the eyes, his face not two feet from mine.

It was nice out, temperature around sixty-five, and the light was still good enough to see perfectly well. I don't know just what I thought I might see, but of course it was Uncle Ira, the same Mr. Lentz I'd known as a kid, delivering an evening paper to the bank every night. He was head teller then—he's retired now—and was always urging me to bank my huge profits from the newspaper route. Now he looked just about the same, except that it was fifteen years later and his hair was white. He's big, well over six feet, a little shambling in his gait now, but still a vigorous, shrewd-eyed, nice old man. And this was him, no one else, standing there on the lawn in the early evening, and I began to feel scared about Wilma.

We chatted about nothing much—local politics, the weather, business—and I studied every line and pore of his face, listened to each tone and inflection of his voice, alert to every move and gesture. You can't really do two things at once, though, and he noticed. "You worried or something, Miles? Seem a little absent-minded tonight."

I smiled and shrugged. "Just taking my work home with me, I guess."

"Mustn't do that, boy; I never did. Forgot all about the bank the minute I put my hat on at night. 'Course you don't get to be president that way." He grinned. "But the president's dead now, and I'm still alive."

Hell, it was Uncle Ira, every hair, every line of his face, each word, movement, and thought, and I felt like a fool. Becky and Wilma came out of the house and sat down on the porch glider, and I waved to them, then walked on up to the house.

CHAPTER

TWO

Wilma sat waiting on the glider with Becky, smiling pleasantly till I reached the porch, then she said quietly, "I'm glad you've come, Miles."

"Hello, Wilma; nice to see you." I sat down on the wide porch rail, facing them, my back against the pillar.

Wilma watched me questioningly, then glanced out at her uncle, who'd begun puttering around the lawn again. "Well?" she said.

I glanced at Ira too, then looked at Wilma. I nodded. "It's him, Wilma. It's your uncle, all right."

She just nodded, as though expecting exactly that answer. "It's not," she murmured, but she said it quietly—not arguing, just asserting a fact.

"Well," I said, leaning my head back against the pillar, "let's take this a little at a time. After all, you could hardly be fooled; you've lived with him for years. How do you know he isn't Uncle

Ira, Wilma? How is he different?"

For a moment her voice shot up, high and pan-icky. "That's just *it!*" But she quieted down instantly, leaning toward me. "Miles, there *is* no difference you can actually see. I'd hoped you might find one, when Becky told me you were here—that you'd see *some* sort of difference. But of course you can't, because there isn't any to see. Look at him."

We all glanced out at the lawn again; Uncle Ira was idly kicking with the side of his foot at a weed or pebble or something imbedded in the lawn. "Every lit-tle move, everything about him is exactly like Ira's." Her face still red-cheeked and round as a circle, but lined now with anxiety, Wilma sat staring at me, eyes intense. "I've been waiting for today," she whispered. "Waiting till he'd get a haircut, and he finally did." Again she leaned toward me, eyes big, her voice a hiss-ing whisper. "There's a little scar on the back of Ira's neck; he had a boil there once, and your father lanced it. You can't see the scar," she whispered, "when he needs a haircut. But when his neck is shaved, you can. Well, today—I've been *waiting* for this!—today he got a haircut—"

I sat forward, suddenly excited. "And the scar's *gone?* You mean—"

"No!" she said, almost indignantly, eyes flashing. "It's *there*—the scar—exactly like Uncle Ira's!"

I didn't answer for a moment. Staring down at the tip of my shoe, I didn't dare glance at Becky, and for a moment I couldn't look at poor Wilma. Then I raised my head, looking her squarely in the eyes, and said it: "Then look, Wilma, he *is* Uncle Ira. Can't you see that? No matter how you feel, he *is*—"

She just shook her head and sat back on the swing. "He's not."

For a moment I was stuck, rattled; I couldn't think of anything else to say. "Where's your Aunt Aleda?"

"It's all right; she's upstairs. Just be sure *he* doesn't hear."

I sat chewing my lip, trying to think. "What about his habits, Wilma?" I said then. "Little mannerisms?"

"All the same as Uncle Ira's. Exactly."

Of course I shouldn't have, but for an instant I lost my patience. "Well, what *is* the difference, then? If there isn't any, how can you tell—" I quieted right down, and tried to be constructive. "Wilma, what about memories? There must be little things only you and Uncle Ira would know."

Pushing her feet against the floor, she began gently moving the glider, gazing out at Uncle Ira, who was staring up at a tree now, as though wondering if it didn't need pruning. "I've tested that, too," she said quietly. "Talked to him about when I was a child." She sighed, trying uselessly, and knowing it was useless, to make me understand.

"Once, years ago, he took me with him into a hardware store. There was a miniature door, set in a little frame, standing on the counter, an advertisement for some kind of lock, I think. It had little hinges, a little doorknob, even a tiny brass knocker. Well, I wanted it, of course, and raised a fuss when I couldn't have it. He remembers that. All about it. What I said, what the clerk said, what he said. Even the name of the store, and it's been gone for years. He even remembers things I'd forgotten completely—a cloud we saw late one Saturday afternoon, when he called for me at the movie after the matinee. It was shaped like a rabbit. Oh, he remembers, all right—everything. Just as Uncle Ira would have."

I'm a general practitioner, not a psychiatrist, and I

was out of my depth and knew it. For a few moments I just sat staring down at the interlaced fingers and the backs of my hands, listening to the quiet creak of the glider.

Then I made one more try, talking quietly, and as persuasively as I could, remembering not to talk down to Wilma and that whatever might have happened to it, her brain was a good one. "Look, Wilma, I'm on your side; my business is people in trouble. This is trouble and needs fixing, and you know that as well as I do, and I'm going to find a way to help you. Now, listen to me. I don't expect you, or ask you, to suddenly agree that this has all been a mistake, that it's really Uncle Ira after all, and you don't know what could have happened to you. I mean I don't expect you to stop feeling *emotionally* that this isn't your uncle. But I do want you to *realize* he's your uncle, no matter what you feel, and that the trouble is inside *you*. It's absolutely impossible for two people to look exactly alike, no matter what you've read in stories or seen in the movies. Even identical twins can always be told apart—always—by their intimates. No one could possibly impersonate your Uncle Ira for more than a moment, without you, Becky, or even me, seeing a million differences. Realize that, Wilma, think about it and get it into your head, and you'll *know* the trouble is inside you. And then we'll be able to do something about it."

I sat back against the porch column—I'd shot my wad—and waited for an answer.

Still swinging gently, her foot pushing rhythmically against the floor, Wilma sat thinking about what I'd just said. Then—eyes staring absently off across the porch—she pursed her lips, and slowly shook her head no.

"*Listen*, Wilma." I spat the words out, leaning far

forward, holding her eyes. "Your Aunt *Aleda* would know! Can't you see that? She couldn't be fooled, of all people! What does *she* say? Have you talked with her, told her about this?"

Wilma just shook her head again, turning to stare across the porch at nothing.

"Why not?"

She turned slowly back toward me; for a moment her eyes stared into mine, then suddenly the tears were running down her plump, twisted face. "Because— Miles—she's not my Aunt Aleda, either!" For an instant, mouth open, she stared at me in absolute horror; then, if you can scream in a whisper, that's what she did. "Oh, my *God*, Miles, am I going crazy? *Tell* me, Miles, tell me; don't spare me, I've got to *know!*" Becky was holding Wilma's hand, squeezing it between her own, her face contorted in an agony of compassion.

I deliberately smiled into Wilma's eyes, exactly as though I knew what I was talking about. "No," I said firmly, "you're not." I grinned and reached forward to lay my hand over hers, clenched on the arm of the glider. "Even these days, Wilma, it isn't as easy to go crazy as you might think."

Making her voice almost calm, Becky said, "I've always heard that if you think you're losing your mind, you're not."

"There's a lot of truth in that," I said, though there isn't. "But, Wilma, you don't have to be losing your mind by a long shot to need psychiatric help. So what? Nowadays, that's nothing, and plenty of people have been help—"

"You don't understand." She sat staring at Uncle Ira, her voice dull and withdrawn now. Then, giving Becky's hand a squeeze in thanks, she withdrew her own hand, and turned to me, no longer crying, and her voice was quiet and firm.

"Miles, he looks, sounds, acts, and remembers exactly like Ira. On the outside. But *inside* he's different. His responses"—she stopped, hunting for the word—"aren't *emotionally* right, if I can explain that. He remembers the past, in detail, and he'll smile and say, 'You were sure a cute youngster, Willy. Bright one, too,' just the way Uncle Ira did. But there's something *missing*, and the same thing is true of Aunt Aleda, lately." Wilma stopped, staring at nothing again, face intent, wrapped up in this, then she continued. "Uncle Ira was a father to me, from infancy, and when he talked about my childhood, Miles, there was—always —a special look in his eyes that meant he was remembering the wonderful quality of those days for him. Miles, that look, 'way in back of the eyes, is gone. With this—*this* Uncle Ira, or whoever or whatever he is, I have the feeling, the absolutely certain *knowledge*, Miles, that he's talking by rote. That the facts of Uncle Ira's memories are all in his mind in every last detail, ready to recall. But the emotions are not. There *is* no emotion—none—only the pretense of it. The words, the gestures, the tones of voice, everything else—but not the feeling."

Her voice was suddenly firm and commanding: "Miles, memories or not, appearances or not, possible or impossible, that is not my Uncle Ira."

There was nothing more to say now, and Wilma knew that as well as I did. She stood up, smiling, and said, "We'd better break this up or"—she nodded toward the lawn—"he'll begin wondering."

I was still confused. "Wondering what?"

"Wondering," she said patiently, "if I don't suspect." Then she held out her hand, and I took it. "You've helped me, Miles, whether you know it or not, and I don't want you to worry too much about me." She turned to Becky. "Or you either." She grinned—"I'm tough; you both know that. And I'll be all right. And if you want me to see your psychiatrist, Miles, I will."

I nodded, said I'd make an appointment for her with Dr. Manfred Kaufman, in San Rafael, the best man I know of, and that I'd phone her in the morning. I muttered some nonsense about relaxing, taking it easy, not worrying, and so on, and Wilma smiled gently and put her hand on my arm the way a woman does when she forgives a man for failing her. Then she thanked Becky for coming over, said she wanted to get to bed early, and I told Becky I'd drive her home.

Going down the walk toward the car, we passed Uncle Ira, and I said, "'Night, Mr. Lentz."

"'Night, Miles; come again." He grinned at Becky, but still speaking to me, said, "Nice having Becky back again, isn't it?" and all but winked.

"Sure is." I smiled, and Becky murmured good night.

In the car I asked Becky if she'd like to do something, have dinner somewhere, maybe, but I wasn't surprised when she wanted to get home.

She lived about three blocks from my house in a big, white, old-fashioned frame house that her father had been born in. When we stopped at the curb, Becky said, "Miles, what do you think—will she be all right?"

I hesitated, then shrugged. "I don't know. I'm a doctor, according to my diploma, but I don't really know what Wilma's trouble is. I could start talking psychiatrical jargon, but the truth is that it's out of my line, and in Mannie Kaufman's."

"Well, do you think he can help her?"

Sometimes there's a limit to how truthful you should be, and I said, "Yes. If anyone can help her, Mannie's the boy to do it. I think he can help her." But I didn't really know.

At Becky's door, without any advance planning or even thinking about it beforehand, I said, "Tomorrow night?" and Becky nodded absently, still thinking about Wilma, and said, "Yes. Around eight?" and I said, "Fine. I'll call for you." You'd think we'd been seeing each other for months; we simply picked right up where we'd left off years earlier; and, walking back to my car, it occurred to me that I was more relaxed and at peace with the world than I'd been in a long, long time.

Maybe that sounds heartless; maybe you think I should have been worrying about Wilma, and in a way I was, far back in my mind. But a doctor learns, because he has to, not to worry actively about patients until the worrying can do some good; meanwhile, they have to be walled off in a quiet compartment of the mind. They don't teach that at medical school, but it's as important as your stethoscope. You've even got to be able to lose a patient, and go on back to your office and treat a cinder in the eye with absolute attention. And if you can't do it, you give up medicine. Or specialize.

I had dinner at Dave's Diner, sitting at a small side table, and noticed the restaurant wasn't at all crowded, and wondered why. Then I went on home, got into pajama pants, and lay in bed reading a paperback mystery, hoping the phone wouldn't ring.

CHAPTER

THREE

Next morning when I got to my office, a patient was waiting, a quiet little woman in her forties who sat in the leather chair in front of my desk, hands folded in her lap over her purse, and told me she was perfectly sure her husband wasn't her husband at all. Her voice calm, she said he looked, talked, and acted exactly the way her husband always had—and they'd been married eighteen years—but that it simply wasn't him. It was Wilma's story all over again, except for the actual details, and when she left I phoned Mannie Kaufman, and made two appointments.

I'll cut this short; by Tuesday of the following week, the night of the Marin General Hospital staff meeting, I'd sent five more patients to Mannie. One was a bright, levelheaded young lawyer I knew fairly well, who was convinced that the married sister he lived with wasn't really his sister, though the woman's own husband obviously still thought so. There were the mothers of three high-school girls, who arrived at my office in a body to tell me, tearfully, that the girls were being laughed at because they insisted their English teacher was actually an impostor who resembled the real teacher exactly. A nine-year-old boy came in with his grandmother, with whom he was now living, because he became hysterical at the sight of his mother who, he said, wasn't his mother at all.

Mannie Kaufman was waiting for me when I arrived, a little early for a change, at the staff meeting. I parked in the hospital lot, and as I set the brake somebody called to me from a parked car down the line. I got out, and walking toward it saw that it was Mannie and Doc Carmichael, another Marin psychiatrist, in the front seat. Ed Pursey, one of my Mill Valley competitors, was in the back seat. Mannie had the door on his side open, and was sitting sideways, his feet out of the car, heels hooked on the bottom ledge. Elbows on his knees, he was leaning forward, hands clasped. He's a dark, nervous, good-looking man; looks like an intelligent football player. Carmichael and Pursey are older, and look more like doctors.

"What the hell's going on in Mill Valley?" Mannie said as I walked up. He glanced at Ed Pursey in the back seat to show he was included in the question, so I knew Ed must have been having some cases, too.

"It's a new hobby over our way," I said, leaning an arm on the open door. "A cinch to replace jogging."

"Well, it's the first contagious neurosis I ever ran into," Mannie said; he was half laughing, half mad. "But, by God, you've got a real epidemic. And if it keeps up you'll kill our racket; we don't know what to do with these people. Right, Charley?" He glanced over his shoulder at Carmichael, at the wheel of the car, who frowned a little. Carmichael upholds the dignity of local psychiatry, while Mannie has the brains.

"Most unusual series of cases," Carmichael said judiciously.

"Well"—I shrugged—"psychiatry is in its infancy, of course. The backward stepchild of medicine, and naturally you two can't—"

"No fooling, Miles; these cases have got me stopped." Mannie looked up at me speculatively, one eye narrowed. "You know what I'd say about any one of these cases, if it weren't absolutely impossible? The Lentz woman, for example? I'd say there was no delusion at all. From every indication I know anything about, I'd say she's not particularly neurotic, at least not in that respect. I'd say she doesn't belong in my office, that her worry is external and real. I'd say—just judging from the patient, of course—that she's right and that her uncle actually is not her uncle. Except that that's impossible." Mannie looked at me curiously, and added, "But it's equally impossible for a total of nine people in Mill Valley to suddenly and simultaneously acquire a virtually identical delusion; right, Charley? Yet that's exactly what seems to have happened."

Charley Carmichael didn't answer, and no one else said anything for a moment. Then Ed Pursey sighed, and said, "I had another this afternoon. Man about fifty. Been a patient of mine for years. Has a daughter, twenty-five. Now she isn't his daughter, he says. Same kind of case." He shrugged and spoke to the front seat. "Shall I send him over to one of you guys?"

Neither of them answered for a moment, then Mannie said, "I don't know. Do what you want. I know I can't help him if he's like the others. Maybe Charley doesn't feel so hopeless."

Carmichael said, "You might send him over; I'll do what I can. But Mannie is right; these are certainly not typical cases of delusion."

"Or anything else," said Mannie.

"Maybe we should try a little blood-letting," I said.

"By god, you might as well," said Mannie.

It was time to go in, and they got out of the car, and we all walked into the hospital. The meeting was as fascinating as usual; we heard a speaker, a university professor who was rambling and dull, and I wished I were with Becky, or at home, or even watching TV. After the meeting, Mannie and I talked a little more, standing in the dark beside my car, but there really wasn't anything more to say, and finally Mannie said, "Well, keep in touch, will you, Miles? We've got to work this out." I said I would, got into my car, and drove on home.

I'd seen Becky at least every other night all the past week, but not because there was anything building up between us. It was just better than hanging around the pool hall, playing solitaire, or collecting stamps. She was a pleasant, comfortable way of spending some evenings, nothing more, and that suited me fine. Wednesday night, when I called for her, we decided on the movies. I called telephone-answering, told Maud Crites, who was on that night, that I was heading for the Sequoia theater, over in Corte Madera, that I was switching my practice entirely to abortions, invited her around as my first patient, and she giggled happily. Then we went on out to the car.

"You look great," I said to Becky, as we walked toward my car, parked at the curb. She did, too; she had on a gray suit with a sort of spray of flowers worked into the material in silver, and running up onto one shoulder.

"Thanks." Becky got into the car, then grinned at me, sort of lazily and happily. "I feel good when I'm with you, Miles," she said. "More at ease than with anyone else. I think it's because we've each been divorced."

I nodded and started the car; I knew what she meant. It was wonderful to be free, but just the same, the breakup of something that wasn't intended to turn out that way leaves you a little shaken, and not too sure of yourself, and I knew I was lucky to have run into Becky. Because we'd each been through the same mill, and it meant I had a woman to go out with on a nice even keel, with none of the unspoken pressures and demands that gradually accumulate between a man and a woman, ordinarily. With anyone else, I knew we'd have been building toward some sort of inevitable climax: marriage, or an affair, or a bustup. But Becky was just what the doctor ordered, and driving along now through the cool fall evening, I felt fine.

We parked in the big lot, and at the box office as I bought our tickets the girl said, "Thanks, Doc: just check in with Gerry," meaning she'd relay any call that came in for me if I'd tell the manager where we were sitting. We bought popcorn in the lobby, walked in, and sat down.

We were lucky; we saw half the picture. Sometimes I think I've seen half of more movies than anyone else alive, and my mind is cluttered with vague, never-to-be-answered wonderings about how certain movies turned out, and how others began. Gerry Montizambert, the manager, was leaning into our aisle, beckoning to me, and I muttered a blasphemy to Becky—it was a good picture, called *Time and Again*, about a guy who finds a way to visit the past—then we pushed our way out past fifty people, each of them equipped with three knees.

As we came out into the lobby, Jack Belicec stepped forward from the popcorn stand and came toward us, smiling apologetically. "Sorry, Miles," he said, glancing at Becky to include her in the apology. "Hate to spoil your movie."

"That's okay. What's the trouble, Jack?"

He didn't answer, but walked forward to hold the outer doors open for us, and I knew he didn't want to talk in the lobby, so we walked on out to the sidewalk, and he followed. But outside as we stopped just past the overhead lights from the marquee, he still wouldn't get to the point. "No one's sick, Miles; it isn't that. Don't know if you could even call it an emergency, exactly. But—I'd certainly like you to come out tonight."

I like Jack. He's a writer, and a good one, I think; I've read one of his books. But I was a little annoyed; this kind of thing happened so often. All day people will wait around, thinking about calling the doctor, but deciding not to, deciding to wait, hoping it won't be necessary. But then it gets dark, and there's something about night that makes them decide that maybe they'd better have the doctor after all. "Well, Jack," I said, "if it's not an emergency, if it's anything that can wait till morning, then why not do that?" I nodded toward Becky. "It's not just my evening, but—You two know each other, by the way?"

Becky smiled, and said, "Yes," and Jack said, "Sure, I know Becky; her dad, too." He frowned, and stood there on the walk thinking for a moment. Then he glanced from me to Becky, including us both in what he was saying. "Look; bring Becky along, if she'd like to come. Might be a good idea; might help my wife." He smiled wryly. "I don't say she'll like what she'll see, but it'll be a lot more interesting than any movie, I'll promise you that."

I glanced at Becky, she nodded, and since Jack is no fool, I didn't ask any more questions. "All right," I said, "let's go in my car so we can talk. I'll drive you back to pick up yours when we're through."

We sat three in the front seat, and on the way— Jack lives in what is still almost country just outside Mill Valley—he didn't offer any more information, and I assumed he had a reason. Jack's a thin-faced intense sort of man, with prematurely white hair. He's about forty years old, I'd say, an intelligent man of good sense and judgment. I knew that, because some months ago his wife was sick and he'd called me in. She had a sudden high fever, extreme lassitude, and I diagnosed it, finally, as Rocky Mountain spotted fever. I wasn't happy about that. You could practice medicine in California for a long time and never run across Rocky Mountain spotted fever, and it was hard to see how she could have caught it. But I didn't see what else it could be, and that's what I advised treatment for, starting at once. I had to tell Jack, though, that I'd never seen a case before, and that if he wanted other opinions he must feel free to get them. But I added that I was as sure of my diagnosis as I thought anyone else around could be of his, and that a conflicting opinion just then —uncertainness on anyone's part—wouldn't be so good. Jack listened, asked some questions, thought about it, then told me to go ahead and treat his wife, which I did. A month later she was well, and baking cookies; Jack brought me a batch at the office. So I respected him; he knew how to make a decision; and I waited, now, till he was ready to talk.

We passed the black-and-white city limits sign, and Jack pointed ahead. "Turn left on the dirt road, if you remember, Miles. It's the green house on the hill."

I nodded, and swung onto the road, shifting for the climb.

He said, "Stop a minute, will you, Miles? I want to ask you something."

I pulled to the edge of the road, set the brake, and turned to him, leaving the engine running.

He took a deep breath, and said, "Miles, there are certain things a doctor has to report when he runs into them, aren't there?"

It was as much a statement as a question, and I just nodded.

"A contagious disease, for example," he went on, as though thinking out loud, "or a gunshot wound, or a dead body. Well, Miles"—he turned to stare out the window on his side—"do you always have to report them? Is there ever a case, I mean, when a doctor might feel justified in overlooking the rules?"

I shrugged. "Depends," I said; I didn't know how to answer him.

"On what?"

"On the doctor, I suppose. And the particular case. What's up, Jack?"

"I can't tell you yet; I've got to know the answer to this first." Staring out his window, he thought for a moment, then turned to look at me. "Maybe you can answer this. Can you imagine a case, any kind of case, a gunshot wound, for example, where the rules or the law or whatever it was, required you to report it? And where you'd get into real trouble if you didn't report it and were found out—maybe even lose your license?

Can you imagine any set of circumstances where you might gamble your reputation, ethics, and license, and not turn in a report, just the same?"

I shrugged again. "I don't know, Jack; I guess so. I guess I could dream up some sort of situation where I'd forget the rules, if it were important enough and I felt I ought to." I was suddenly irritated at all the mystery. "I don't know, Jack; what are you getting at? This is all too vague, and I don't want you to get the idea that I'm promising a thing. If you've got something up at your house that I ought to report, I'll probably report it; that's all I can tell you."

Jack smiled. "All right; that's good enough. I think maybe you'll decide not to report this one." He nodded toward his house—"Let's go on up."

I pulled out into the road again, and the headlights caught a figure, maybe a hundred yards ahead, walking toward us. It was a woman, still wearing an apron, arms huddled across her chest, hands cupping her elbows; it gets cool here, in the evenings. Then I saw it was Theodora, Jack's wife.

I pulled toward her slowly, then stopped beside her. She said, "Hello, Miles," then spoke to Jack, looking into the car through my open window. "I couldn't stay up there alone, Jack. I just couldn't; I'm sorry."

He nodded. "I should have brought you along; it was stupid of me not to."

Opening the car door, I leaned forward to let Theodora into the back seat, then Jack introduced her to Becky, and we drove on up to the house.

CHAPTER

FOUR

J ack's is a green frame house sitting by itself on the side of a hill, and the garage is a part of the basement. The garage was empty, the door open, and Jack motioned me to drive right in. We got out of the car then, Jack snapped on a light, closed the garage door, then opened a door leading into the basement proper, motioning us to walk on in ahead of him.

We stepped into an ordinary basement: an old-style laundry tub, a washing machine, a wooden sawhorse, stacked newspapers, and against one wall, on the floor, some cardboard cartons and several used paint cans. Jack walked past us across the room to another door, then stopped, turned toward us, his hand on the doorknob. He had a pretty good second-hand billiard table in there, I knew; he'd told me he used it a lot, just knocking the balls around by himself, doing a lot of his writing in his head. Now he looked at Becky, glancing at his wife, too. "Get hold of yourself," he said, then walked in, pulled the chain on the overhead light, and we followed after him.

The light over a billiard table is designed to light up the table surface brilliantly. It hangs low so it won't shine in your eyes as you play, and it leaves the ceiling in darkness. This one had a rectangular shade to confine the light to the table top only, and the rest of the room was left in semigloom. I couldn't see Becky's face very clearly, but I heard her gasp. Lying on the bright green table top under the sharp light of the 150-watt bulb, and covered with the rubberized sheet Jack kept on the billiard table, lay what was unmistakably a body. I turned to look at Jack, and he said, "Go ahead; pull it off."

I was irritated; this worried and scared me, and there was too damn much mystery to suit me; it occurred to me that the writer in Jack was laying on the dramatics a little heavily. I grabbed the rubber sheet, yanked it off, and tossed it to a corner of the table. Lying on the green felt, on its back, was the naked body of a man. It was maybe five feet ten inches tall— it isn't too easy to judge heights, looking down on a body that way. He was white, the skin very pale in the brilliant shadowless light, and at one and the same time, it looked unreal and theatrical, and yet it was intensely, overly real. The body was slim, maybe 140 pounds, but well-nourished and well-muscled. I couldn't judge the age, except that he wasn't old. The eyes were open, staring directly up into the overhead light, in a way that made your own eyes smart. They were blue, and very clear. There was no wound visible, and no other obvious cause of death. I walked over beside Becky, slipped my arm under hers, and turned to Jack. "Well?"

He shook his head, refusing to comment. "Keep

looking. Examine it. Notice anything strange?"

I turned back to the body on the table. I was getting more and more irritated. I didn't like this; there *was* something strange about this dead man on the table, but I couldn't tell what, and that only made me angrier. "Come on, Jack"—I looked at him again. "I don't see anything but a dead man. Let's cut out the mystery; what's it all about?"

Again he shook his head, frowning pleadingly. "Miles, take it easy. Please. I don't want to tell you my impression of what's wrong; I don't want to influence you. If it's there to see, I want you to find it yourself, first. And if it isn't, if I'm imagining things, I want to know that, too. Bear with me, Miles," he said gently. "Take a good look at that thing."

I studied the corpse, walking slowly around the table, stopping to look down at it from various angles, Jack, Becky, and Theodora stepping aside out of my way as I moved. "All right," I said presently, and reluctantly, apologizing to Jack with the tone of my voice. "There *is* something funny about it. You're not imagining things. Or if you are, so am I." For maybe half a minute longer I stood staring down at what lay on the table. "Well, for one thing," I said finally, "you don't often see a body like this, dead or alive. In a way, it reminds me of a few tubercular patients I've seen— those who've been in sanitariums nearly all their lives." I looked around at them all. "You can't live an ordinary life without picking up a few scars, a few nicks here and there. But these sanitarium patients never had a chance to get any; their bodies were unused. And that's how this one looks"—I nodded at the pale, motionless body under the light. "It's not tubercular, though. It's a well-built, healthy body; those are good muscles. But it never played football or hockey, never fell on a cement stair, never broke a bone. It looks...unused. That what you mean?"

Jack nodded. "Yeah. What else?"

"Becky, you all right?" I glanced across the table at her.

"Yes." She nodded, biting at her lower lip.

"The face," I said, answering Jack. I stood looking down at that face, waxy-white, absolutely still and motionless, the china-clear eyes staring. "It's not—immature, exactly." I wasn't sure how to say this. "Those are good bones; it's an adult face. But it looks"—I hunted for the word, and couldn't find it—"vague. It looks—"

Jack interrupted, his voice tense and eager; he was actually smiling a little. "Did you ever see them make medals?"

"Medals?"

"Yeah, fine medals. Medallions."

"No."

"Well, for a really fine job, in hard metal," Jack said, settling into his explanation, "they make two impressions." I didn't know what he was talking about or why. "First, they take a die and make impression number one, giving the blank metal its first rough shape. Then they stamp it with die number two, and it's the second die that gives it the details: the fine lines and delicate modeling you see in a really good medallion. They have to do it that way because that second die, the one with the details, couldn't force its way into smooth metal. You have to give it that first rough shape with die number one." He stopped, looking from me to Becky, to see if we were following him.

"So?" I said a little impatiently.

"Well, usually a medallion shows a face. And when you look at it after die number one, the face isn't *finished.* It's all there, all right, but the details that give it character aren't." He stared at me. "Miles, that's what this face looks like. It's all there; it has lips, a nose, eyes, skin, and bone structure underneath. But there are no lines, no *details*, no character. It's unformed. Look at it!" His voice rose a notch. "It's like a blank face, waiting for the final finished face to be stamped onto it!"

He was right. I'd never seen a face like that before in my life. It wasn't flabby; you certainly couldn't say that. But somehow it was formless, characterless. It really wasn't a face; not yet. There was no *life* to it, it wasn't marked by experience; that's the only way I can explain it. "Who is he?" I said.

"I don't know." Jack walked to the doorway and nodded out at the basement and the staircase leading upstairs. "There's a little closet under the stairway; it's walled in with plywood to make a little storage space. It's half full of old junk: clothes in cardboard boxes, burned-out electrical appliances, an old vacuum cleaner, an iron, some lamps, stuff like that. We hardly ever open it. And there are some old books in there, too. I found him in there; I was hunting for a reference I needed, and thought it might be in one of those books. He was lying there, on top of the cartons, just the way you see him now; scared me stiff. I backed out like a cat in a doghouse; got a hell of a bump on the head"— he touched his scalp. "Then I went back and pulled him out. I thought he might still be alive, I couldn't tell. Miles, how soon does rigor mortis set in?"

"Oh—eight to ten hours."

"Feel him," said Jack. In a way he was enjoying himself, as a man will who's made a big promise and is living up to it.

I picked up an arm from the table, by the wrist; it

was loose and flexible. It didn't even feel clammy, or particularly cold.

"No rigor mortis," Jack said. "Right?"

"That's right," I said, "but rigor mortis isn't invariable. There are certain conditions—" I stopped talking; I didn't know what to make of this.

"If you want," said Jack, "you can turn him over, but you won't find any wounds in the back, and there are none in the hair. Not a sign of what killed him."

I hesitated, but legally I couldn't touch this body, and I picked up the rubber sheet, and tossed it over the body again, half covering it. "All right," I said. "Where to, now? Upstairs?"

"Yeah." Jack nodded at the doorway, and stood with his hand on the light chain till we'd all filed out.

Up in the living room, Theodora politely asked us to sit down, went around turning on lamps, then went into the kitchen and came back in a moment without her apron. She sat down in a big easy chair, Becky and I were on the chesterfield, and Jack was sitting by the window in a wooden rocking chair, looking down on the town. Almost the whole front wall of his living room is a single sheet of plate glass, and you could see the lights of the entire town scattered through the hills; it's a nice room.

"Want a drink or anything?" Jack said then.

Becky shook her head, and I said, "No thanks; you folks go ahead, though."

Jack said no, glancing at his wife, and she shook her head. Then he said, "We called you, Miles, because you're a doctor, but also because you're a guy who can face facts. Even when the facts aren't what they ought to be. You're not a man to knock yourself out trying to talk black into white, just because it's more comfortable. Things are what they are with you, as we have reason to know."

I shrugged, and didn't say anything.

"You got anything more to say about this body downstairs?" Jack asked.

I sat there for a moment or so, fiddling with a button on my coat, then made up my mind to say it. "Yeah," I said, "I have. This doesn't make sense, it makes no sense at all, but I'd give a lot to perform an autopsy on that body, because you know what I think I'd find?" I glanced around the room—at Jack, Theodora, then Becky—and no one answered; they just sat there waiting. "I think I'd find no cause of death at all. I think I'd find every organ in as perfect condition as the body is externally. Everything in perfect working order, ready to go."

I let them think about that for a moment, then gave them some more; I felt utterly foolish saying it, and utterly certain I was right. "That isn't all. I think that when I opened the stomach, there'd be nothing inside. Not a crumb, not a particle of food, digested or undigested; nothing. Empty as a newborn baby's. And if I opened the bowel, the same thing: no waste, not a bit. Nothing at all. Why?" I glanced around at them again. "Because I don't believe that that body downstairs ever died. There is no cause of death, because it never died. And it never died because it's never been alive." I shrugged, and sat back on the chesterfield. "There you are. That far out enough for you?"

"Yeah," Jack said, slowly and emphatically nodding his head, the women silently watching us. "That's exactly nutty enough for me. I only wanted it confirmed."

"Becky"—I turned to look at her—"what do you think?"

She shook her head, frowning, then sighed. "I'm —stunned. But I think I would like that drink, after all. Bourbon and soda?"

We all smiled then, and Jack started to get up, but Theodora said, "I'll get them," and stood. "One for everyone?" she asked, and we all said yes.

Then we sat waiting, changing position, glancing out the window, till Theodora came back and handed drinks around. We each took a sip, then Jack said, "That's exactly what I think, and so does Theodora. And the thing is, I didn't tell her anything about my impressions. I let her look at that thing, and form her own opinion, just like I did with you, Miles. She's the one who first made the comparison with the medallions; we saw them making medallions once, in Washington." Jack sighed, and shook his head. "We've talked and thought about this all day, Miles; then decided to call you."

"You tell anyone else?"

"No."

"Why didn't you call the police?"

"I don't know." Jack looked at me, a little smile around his mouth. "You want to call them?"

"No."

"Why not?"

Then I smiled, too. "I don't know. But I don't."

"Yeah." Jack nodded in agreement, then we all sat there for several moments, sipping our drinks. Jack rattled the ice idly in his glass and, staring down at it, said slowly, "I have a feeling that this is a time to do something more than call the police. That this isn't a time to pass the buck, and let someone else do the worrying. What exactly could the police do? This isn't just a body, and we know it. It's"—he shrugged, his face somber—"something terrible. Something... I don't know what." He looked up from his glass, glancing around at us all. "I only know, and somehow I'm certain of this, that we mustn't make a mistake here. That there is some one thing—the wise thing, the single correct thing, the one and only thing to do—and if we fail to do it, if we guess wrong, something terrible is going to happen."

I said, "Do what, for instance?"

"I don't know." Jack turned away to stare out the window for a moment. Then he looked back at us, and smiled a little. "I have a terrible urge to... call the President at the White House direct, or the head of the Army, the FBI, the Marines, or the Cavalry, or something." He shook his head in smiling amusement at himself, then the smile faded. "Miles, what I mean is, I want *somebody*—exactly the right person, whoever he is—to realize from the very start how important this is. And I want him, or them, to do whatever should be done, without a mistake. And the thing is that whoever I got in touch with, if he'd even listen to or believe me, might be exactly the wrong person, somebody who'd do exactly the worst thing possible. Whatever that might be. But I do know this isn't something for the police. This is—" He shrugged, realizing he was repeating himself, and stopped talking.

"I know," I said. "I have the same feeling, the feeling that the world better hope we handle this right." In medicine sometimes, on a puzzling case, an answer or a clue will pop up out of nowhere; the subconscious mind at work, I suppose. I said, "Jack, how tall are you?"

"Five ten."

"Exactly?"

"Yeah. Why?"

"How tall would you say the body downstairs is?"

He looked at me for a moment, then said, "Five ten."

"And what do you weigh?"

"One forty." He nodded. "Yeah, just about what that body downstairs weighs. You've hit it; it's my size and build. Doesn't especially look like me, though."

"Or anyone else. You got an ink pad in the house?"

He turned to his wife. "Have we?"

"A what?"

"An ink pad. The kind you use for rubber stamps."

"Yes." Theodora got up and crossed the room to a desk. "There's one in here somewhere." She found and brought out an ink pad, and Jack went over, took it, then opened another drawer and brought out a sheet of stationery.

I went over to the desk and so did Becky. Jack inked the ends of all five fingers of his right hand, then held out his hand to me. I took it, then pressed the fingers, carefully rolling each one on the sheet of paper, getting a full set of clean, sharp prints. Then I picked up stamp pad and paper. "You girls want to come?" I nodded at the door.

They looked at each other; they didn't want to go back to that billiard table, and they didn't want to stay up here waiting, either. Becky said, "No, but I'm going to," and Theodora nodded.

Downstairs, Jack turned on the light over the billiard table. It swung a little, and I reached out to the shade to steady it. But my fingers trembled, and I only made it worse. The shade still swung in a tiny half-inch arc, the light spilling off over the edge of the table, then retreating to the open eyes of the body, leaving the smooth forehead in semidark for an instant. It gave you the impression that the body was moving a little, and I picked up the right wrist, concentrating on that, not looking at the face. I inked the ends of all five fingers, then I laid the sheet of paper containing Jack's fingerprints on the wide table ledge, beside the body's right hand. I brought the hand up, laid it on the white sheet, and rolling each finger, I took an impression of them all, directly under Jack's prints, then lifted the hand from the paper.

Becky actually moaned when we saw the prints, and I think we all felt sick. Because it's one thing to speculate about a body that's never been alive, a blank. But it's something very different, something that touches whatever is primitive deep in your brain, to have that speculation proved. There were no prints; there were five absolutely smooth, solidly black circles. I wiped the ink off the fingers fairly well, and we all bent over, huddled in a circle under the swinging light, and looked at the darkened ends of those fingers. They were smooth as a baby's cheek, and Theodora murmured quietly, "Jack, I'll be sick," and he turned to grab her—she was bending at the waist—then helped her upstairs.

Sitting in the living room again, I shook my head, and said to Jack, "You've got the word for it, all right. It's a blank; unfinished, and still waiting for the final impression."

He nodded. "What'll we do? You got any ideas?"

"Yeah"—I sat looking at him for a moment. "But it's only a suggestion, and if you don't want to go through with it, nobody'll blame you, certainly not me."

"What is it?"

"Remember, this is only a suggestion." I leaned

forward on the chesterfield, forearms on my knees, and now I turned to Theodora. "And if *you* don't think you can take this," I said to her, "you'd better not try it, I'm warning you." I looked at Jack again. "Leave it where it is, down on that table. Tonight you'll go to sleep; I'll give you something to take." I glanced at Theodora— "But you stay awake; don't sleep for an instant. Every hour, *if* you can do this, I want you to go downstairs and look at that—body. If you see any hint of a change, hurry upstairs and wake Jack up, right away. Get him out of the house—both of you get out right away—and come right down to my place."

Jack looked at Theodora for a moment, then he said quietly, "I want you to say no, if you don't think you can go through with that."

She sat biting gently at her lip, staring at the rug. Then she looked up, first at me, then turned to Jack. "What would it . . . start looking like? If it started to change?"

No one answered, and after a moment she looked down at the rug, nibbling her lip again, and didn't repeat the question. "Would Jack wake up all right?" Theodora looked at me. "Could I wake him any time?"

"Yes. A slap on the face, and he'll wake right up. Now, listen; even if nothing happens, wake him up if you find you can't stand it. You can both come down to my place for the rest of the night then, if you want."

She nodded, and stared at the rug again. Finally she said, "I guess I could." She looked up at Jack, frowning. "As long as I know I can wake him any time, I guess I could."

"Couldn't we stay with her?" Becky said.

I shrugged. "I don't know. But I don't think so. I think just the people who live here ought to be here; I'm not sure it'll work otherwise. I don't know why I say that, though; it's just a hunch, a feeling. But I think only Jack and Theodora should be here."

Jack nodded, and after glancing at Theodora to confirm this, said, "We'll try it."

We sat then, and talked some more—quite a while, in fact—staring down at the tiny lights of the town in the little valley below. But no one said anything much that hadn't already been said, and around twelve, most of the lights in the town below now out, Becky and I stood up to leave. The Belicecs got their coats, and drove with us to pick up Jack's car. It was parked in the town parking lot, and when we stopped beside their car, and they got out, I repeated to Theodora what I'd said about waking Jack up and beating it out of there if the body in their basement started to alter in any way. I got some half-strength Seconal out of my satchel and gave it to Jack, and told him that one ought to get him to sleep. Then they said good night—Jack smiling a little, Theodora not bothering to try—got into their car, and we waved, and drove on.

In Mill Valley on our way to her house, through the empty streets, Becky said quietly, "There's a connection, isn't there, Miles? Between this and—Wilma's case?"

I glanced at her quickly, but she was staring straight ahead through the windshield. "What do you think?" I said casually. "You think there's a connection?"

"Yes." She didn't look to me for confirmation, but simply nodded as though she were certain. After a moment she added, "Have there been other cases like Wilma's?"

"A few." Watching the asphalt street in the headlight beams, I watched Becky, too, from the corners of my eyes.

But she didn't react, or say anything, for nearly a block. Then we swung into her street, and as I drew the car in to the curb and stopped at her house, she said— still looking straight ahead through the windshield— "Miles, I'd meant to tell you this, after the movie." She took a deep breath. "Ever since yesterday morning," she began slowly, keeping her voice calm, "I've had the feeling that"—she finished in a panicky rush of words —"that my father isn't my father at all!" Darting a horrified glance at the dark, shadowed porch of her home, Becky covered her face with her hands and began to cry.

CHAPTER

FIVE

I don't claim a lot of experience with crying women, but in stories I read, the man always holds the woman close and lets her cry. And it always turns out to have been the wise, understanding thing to do; I've never heard of a single authenticated case where the wise, understanding thing was to distract her with card tricks or tickling her feet. So I was wise and understanding: I held Becky close and let her cry, because I didn't know what else to do or say. After what we'd seen in Jack Belicec's basement tonight, if Becky believed her father was an impostor who resembled her real father exactly, I didn't know how to argue with her.

Anyway, I liked holding Becky. She wasn't a big woman exactly, but she wasn't small, and nothing in her construction had been skimped or neglected. There in my car, on the silent street in front of her home, Becky fitted into my arms very nicely, her cheek on my lapel. I was worried and scared, even panicky, but there was still room for enjoying the warm, alive feel of Becky pressed close.

When the crying tapered off to an occasional sniffle, I said, "How about staying at my place tonight?" The idea was suddenly and astonishingly exciting.

"No." Becky sat up, keeping her head ducked so I couldn't see her face, and began fumbling through her purse. "I'm not frightened, Miles," she said quietly, "just worried." She brought out a handkerchief, and began touching it to the tear marks. "It's as though Dad were sick," she went on. "Just not himself, and—Well, it's just no time for me to leave." She looked at me, and smiled. Suddenly she leaned toward me and quickly kissed me on the mouth, very firmly and warmly. Then she opened her door and slipped out. "'Night, Miles. Phone me in the morning." She walked quickly along the brick path leading to the darkened porch of her home.

I watched her go. I sat staring after her fine full figure, heard the tiny gritting of her shoes on the rough bricks of the path, heard her light steps go quickly up the stairs, and saw her disappear into the gloom of the porch. A pause, the front door opened, then closed behind her. And all the time I was sitting there shaking my head at myself, remembering my thoughts about Becky early in the evening. She was not, after all, turning out to be just a good pal who happened to wear skirts. Put a nice-looking woman you're fond of in your arms, I was realizing, have her weep a little, and you're a cinch to feel pretty tender and protective. Then that feeling starts to get mixed up with sex, and if you're not careful, you've made at least a start toward something I'd meant to avoid for a while. I grinned then, and started the car. So I'd be careful, that's all. With the wreckage of one marriage still around me, I wasn't walking into anything serious just yet. Near the corner at the end of the block, I glanced back at Becky's house, big and white in the faint starlight, and knew that while I liked her fine, and while she was attractive, I could put her out of my mind without much trouble, and I did. I drove on through the quiet town thinking about the Belicecs, up there in their house on the hill.

Jack was asleep now, I was certain, and Theodora was probably in the living room staring down at the town, right now. Most likely she was watching my headlights at this very moment, not knowing it was me. I imagined her sipping coffee, fighting the horror of what lay just under her feet in the billiard room—and building up her nerve to walk down there pretty soon, fumble for the light, then lower her eyes to that staring waxy-white thing on the kelly-green felt of the table.

Some two hours later when the phone rang, my bed lamp was still on; I'd been reading, not expecting I would fall asleep for a while, yet I had, right away. It was three o'clock; reaching out for the phone, I noted the time automatically.

"Hello," I said, and as I spoke I heard the phone at the other end crash down into its cradle. I knew I'd answered at the first ring; no matter how tired I am at night, I always hear and answer the telephone instantly. I said, "Hello!" again, a little louder, jiggling the phone, the way you do, but the line was dead, and I put the phone back. In my father's day a night operator, whose name he'd have known, could have told him who'd called. It would probably have been the only light on her board at that time of night, and she'd have remembered which one it was, because they were calling the doctor. But now we have dial phones, marvelously efficient, saving you a full second or more every time you call, inhumanly perfect, and utterly brainless;

and none of them will ever remember where the doctor is at night, when a child is sick and needs him. Sometimes I think we're refining all humanity out of our lives.

Sitting on the edge of the bed, I began to curse tiredly. I was fed up—with telephones, with events and mysteries, with interrupted sleep, women who bothered me when I only wanted to be left alone, with my own thoughts, with everything. I thought about getting up, but didn't, turned off the light, and was nearly asleep again, when I heard the steps tumbling up the porch stairs, then the quick, liquid peal of the doorbell, always so unexpectedly louder at night, followed instantly by a frantic, rapid tapping on the glass of the front door.

It was the Belicecs: Theodora wild-eyed, her face dough-white, incapable of speech; Jack with furious, dead-calm eyes. We said only the bare words necessary to get Theodora, half carrying her, up the stairs, and onto a guest room bed, a blanket over her, and some sodium amytal in a vein.

Then Jack sat on the edge of the bed and watched her for a long time, twenty minutes maybe, holding her hand flat between his two palms, staring at her face. I sat in my pajamas on the other side of the room, in a big easy chair, till Jack finally looked up at me. Then I nodded my head, and deliberately spoke in a normally loud tone: "She'll sleep for several hours at least, Jack; maybe even till eight or nine in the morning. Then she'll wake up hungry, and she'll be all right."

Jack nodded, accepting that, sat staring at Theodora for several moments longer, then stood up, turning toward the door, and I followed after him.

My living room is big, carpeted in plain gray from wall to wall; the woodwork is painted white, and the room is still furnished in the blue-painted wicker furniture my parents bought for it. It's a large, pleasant room that still retains, I think, some of the simpler, more peaceful feeling of other times. We sat there, Jack and I, across the room from each other, with drinks in our hands, and after a few sips of his, staring down at the floor, Jack began to talk. "Theodora woke me, shaking me by the front of my shirt—I slept with my clothes on—and slapping me so hard my teeth jarred. I heard her"—Jack looked up at me, frowning; he usually chooses his words rather carefully—"not calling me, exactly, but just saying my name in a subdued, desperate kind of moan, 'Jack . . . Jack . . . Jack . . .'"

He shook his head at the memory, bit his lower lip a couple times, then took a deep swallow of his drink. "I came to, and she was hysterical. Didn't say anything. Just stared at me for a second, wild and sort of frantic, then she whirled away, darting across the room to the phone, grabbed it, dialed you, stood waiting for a second, then couldn't stand still, slammed the phone down, and began crying out at me—very softly, as though someone might hear—to get her out of there."

Again Jack shook his head, his cheek quirking in annoyance at himself. "Not thinking, I took her wrist and started leading her down the basement stairs to the garage and the car, and she began to fight me, yanking her arm to get loose, shoving at my shoulder, her face just wild. Miles, I think she'd have raked down my face with her nails if I hadn't let go. We went out the front door then, and down the outside steps. Even at that, she wouldn't come near the garage or basement; she stood well out on the road, away from the house, while I got the car out."

Jack took a swig of his drink and stared at a living room window, shiny black against the night. "I'm not sure what she saw, Miles"—he glanced over at me—"though I can guess, and so can you. But I couldn't take time to go see for myself; I knew I had to get her out of there. And she didn't tell me anything on the way down here. She just sat there, all huddled up and shivering, pressed tight against me—I kept an arm around her—saying, 'Jack, oh, Jack, Jack, Jack.'" For several moments he stared at me somberly. "We proved something, all right, Miles," he said then with quiet bitterness. "The experiment worked, I guess. Now what?"

I didn't know, or try to pretend I did. I just shook my head. "I'd like to get a look at that thing," I murmured.

"Yeah, me too. But I won't leave Theodora alone just now. If she woke up and called, and I didn't answer—the house empty—she'd go out of her mind."

I didn't answer. It's possible—it happens to everyone, in fact—to think through a fairly long series of thoughts in a moment, and that's what I did now. I thought about driving up to Jack's place alone. I imagined myself stopping my car beside that empty house, getting out of the car, in the darkness, then standing there listening to the silence. Then I pictured myself walking ahead into the open garage, shuffling slowly across that dark basement, fumbling along the wall for an unfamiliar light switch. I saw myself actually walking into that pitch-black billiard room, feeling my way across it to the table, knowing what was lying there, and getting closer and closer to it, my palms raised to find it, hoping they'd touch the table and not blunder onto that cool, unalive skin in the dark. I thought of bumping into the table then, finding the light overhead finally; then turning it on, and lowering my eyes to look at—whatever had sent Theodora into shocked hysteria.

And I was ashamed. I didn't want to do what I'd let Theodora do; I didn't want to go up there to that house in the night, not alone.

I was suddenly angry, at myself. In that same second or so of thought, I was finding excuses, telling myself that there wasn't *time* to go up there now; that we had to act, had to do something. And I took my anger and shame out on Jack. "Listen"—I was on my feet, staring furiously across the room at him—"whatever we're going to do about this, we've got to start *doing* it! So what do you say? You got any ideas? What'll we *do*, for God's sake!" I was actually a little hysterical, and knew it.

"I don't know," Jack said slowly. "But we've got to move carefully, make sure we're doing the right thing—"

"You said that! You already said that early this evening, and I agree, I agree! But *what?* We can't sit around forever till the one correct move is finally revealed to us!" I was glaring at Jack, then I forced myself to behave. I thought of something, turned to cross the room rapidly, winking at Jack to let him know I was okay now. Then I picked up the downstairs phone and dialed a number.

The ringing began, and I had to grin; I was getting a little malicious pleasure out of this. When a general practitioner hangs out his little shingle, he knows he's going to be telephoned out of bed for the rest of his life perhaps. In a way he gets used to it, and in a way never does. Because most often the phone late at night is something serious; frightened people to deal with, and everything you do twice as hard; maybe pharmacists to roust out of bed, hospitals to stir into action. And underneath it all, to hide from the patient and his family, are your own night-time fears and doubts about yourself to beat down; because everything depends on you now and nobody else—you're the doctor. The phone at night is no fun, and sometimes it's impossible not to resent those branches of medicine that never, or rarely, have emergency calls.

So when the ringing at the other end of the wire was finally broken, I was grinning, delighted with my mental picture of Dr. Manfred Kaufman, black hair mussed, eyes barely open, wondering who could possibly be phoning. "Hello; Mannie?" I said, when he answered.

"Yeah."

"Listen"—I made my voice exaggeratedly solicitous—"did I wake you up?"

That brought him to life, cursing like a wild man.

"Why, Doctor," I said, "where in the world did you learn such language? From your patients' foul and slimy subconscious, I suppose. How I wish I were a head-doctor, charging seventy-five bucks a throw just to sit and listen and improve my vocabulary. No tiresome night-time calls! No dreary operations! No annoying prescrip—"

"Miles, what the hell do you want? I'm warning you, I'll hang up, and leave the damn phone off the—"

"Okay, okay, Mannie; listen." I was still smiling, but the tone of my voice promised no more bad jokes. "Something has happened, and I've got to see you. Just as quick as possible, and it has to be here, at my place. Get over here as fast as you can; it's important."

Mannie's quick-minded; he gets things fast, and you don't have to repeat or explain. For just an instant he was silent, at the other end of the wire, then he said, "Okay," and hung up.

I was enormously relieved, crossing the room toward my chair and my drink again. In an emergency calling for brains, or almost anything else, Mannie's the first man I'd want on my side, and now he was on his way, and I felt we were getting somewhere. I picked up my drink, ready to sit down, and I actually had my mouth open to speak to Jack, when something happened that you read about often but seldom experience. In a single instant I broke out into a cold sweat, and I stood there stock still for several seconds, paralyzed, and shriveling inside with fear.

What had happened was simple enough; I'd suddenly thought of something. Something had occurred to me, a danger so obvious and terrible that I knew I should have thought of it long since, but I hadn't. And now, terror filling my mind, I knew I hadn't a single second to lose, and I couldn't act fast enough. I was wearing elastic-sided slippers, and I ran to the hall and grabbed up my light topcoat from a chair, shoving my arms into my coat sleeves as I swung toward the front door. I had only one thought, and it was impossible to do anything but act, move, *run*. I'd forgotten all about Jack, forgotten Mannie, as I yanked the front door open and ran out, and down the steps into the night, across the lawn and the sidewalk. At the curb, I had my hand on the door of my car when I remembered that the ignition key was upstairs, and it simply wasn't possible to turn around and go back. I began to run—as hard as I could—and somehow, for no reason I can explain, the sidewalk seemed hampering, seemed to slow me down, and I darted across the grass strip toward the curb; then I was running frantically down the dark and deserted streets of Mill Valley.

For two blocks I saw nothing else moving. The houses lining the street were silent and blank, and the only sounds in the world were the rapid slap-slap of my slippers on the asphalt pavement and the raw gasps of my breathing, which seemed to fill the street. Just ahead now, at the intersection, the pavement lightened, then suddenly brightened, showing every tiny pebble and flaw on its surface in the headlights of an approaching car. I couldn't seem to think, couldn't do anything but run on, straight into that glare of bouncing light, then brakes squealed and rubber shrieked on the pavement and the chrome end of a bumper slapped through the tail of my coat. "You son of a bitch," a male voice savage with fright and anger was shrieking at me. "You crazy bastard!" The voice diminished behind me to a frustrated babble as my pumping legs carried me on into the darkness.

CHAPTER

SIX

I could hardly see when I got to Becky's. My pounding
heart seemed to pile blood behind my eyeballs,
filming my vision, and the whistle of my breath
bounced and echoed between the frame walls of
Becky's home and the house next door. I began testing
each basement window, pushing each one inward with
all my strength, using both hands, then shuffling over
the grass at a jog, to the next. They were all locked. I'd
circled the house, and now I bunched the hem of my
coat around my fist, held it against the glass of the
window, and pushed, increasing the pressure till suddenly it cracked. One piece fell inward, dropped into
the basement, and broke, tinkling, on the floor. From
the hole in the glass, the cracks flared out, the other
broken pieces bulging inward, but still hanging in
place. I was thinking now, and in the faint starlight I
carefully picked out the broken fragments one by one,
dropping them in the grass, widening the hole. Then I

reached in, unlatched the window, opened it, then crawled in feet first, sliding down over the ledge on my belly till my feet found the floor. Pressing against my chest as I slid down, I felt the fountain-pen flashlight I carry in my coat; then, standing in the basement, I turned it on.

The feeble little yard-long beam was wide and diffused, and showed nothing at all beyond a step or two ahead. Slowly I shuffled around that dark, unfamiliar basement, passing bundles of stacked-up old newspapers, a rusting screen door leaning against a cement-block wall, a paint-smeared, saw-marked sawhorse, an old trunk, an old sink and a pile of discarded lead piping, the wooden six-by-six supporting pillars of the basement, a framed dusty group photograph of Becky's high-school graduating class—and I began to get panicky. Time was passing, I wasn't finding what I was certain was here somewhere, and what I had to find if it wasn't already too late.

I tried the old trunk; it was unlocked, and I thrust my arm down into it to the shoulder, stirring around in the old clothes the trunk was filled with, till I knew it contained nothing else. There was nothing among the stacks of old newspapers, or behind the screen door, nothing in an old bookcase I found, its shelves lined with empty, earth-crusted flowerpots. I saw a wooden workbench littered with tools and wood shavings, odds and ends of unused lengths of lumber stacked underneath it. As quietly as possible, I pulled most of that lumber aside, but still I made a good deal of noise; there was nothing under that bench but lumber. I shot the little beam up to the rafters; they were open and exposed, covered with dust and fluff, and there was nothing else on them. Time continued to pass, and I'd searched that whole basement. I didn't know where else to look, and I kept glancing at the windows, afraid I might see the first hint of dawn.

Then I discovered a set of tall cupboards. They were built against an end wall, extending the full width of the basement, and covering it from floor to ceiling. In the weak beam of my flashlight, I'd thought at first that they were the wall itself, and hadn't noticed them. I opened the first set of double doors; the shelves were loaded with canned goods. I opened the next set of doors beside them, and the shelves were dusty and empty, all but the bottom one, no more than an inch from the floor.

There it lay, on that unpainted pine shelf, flat on its back, eyes wide open, arms motionless at its sides; and I got down on my knees beside it. I think it must actually be possible to lose your mind in an instant, and that perhaps I came very close to it. And now I knew why Theodora Belicec lay on a bed in my house in a state of drugged shock, and I closed my eyes tight, fighting to hold on to control of myself. Then I opened them again and looked, holding my mind, by sheer force, in a state of cold and artificial calm.

I've watched a man develop a photograph, a portrait he'd taken of a mutual friend. He dipped the sheet of blank sensitized paper into the solution, slowly swishing it back and forth, in the dim red light of the developing room. Then, underneath that colorless fluid, the image began to reveal itself—dimly and vaguely— yet unmistakably recognizable just the same. This thing, too, lying on its back on that dusty shelf in the feeble orange glow of my flashlight, was an unfinished, underdeveloped, vague and indefinite Becky Driscoll.

The hair, like Becky's, was brown and wavy, and it sprang up from the forehead, wiry and strong, and already there was the beginning of a dip at the center of the hairline, suggesting the widow's peak of Becky Driscoll's head of hair. Under the skin, the bone structure was pushing up; cheekbone and chin, and the modeling around the eyes was beginning to show prominently, as did Becky's. The nose was narrow, flaring into a sudden wideness at the bridge, and I saw that if it widened only a fraction of an inch more, this nose would be a duplicate, precise as a wax cast, of Becky's. The lips formed very nearly the same full, ripe, and — this was horrible — good-looking mouth. At each side of that mouth were appearing the two tiny, nearly invisible grooves of worry that had appeared on Becky Driscoll's face in the past few years.

It is impossible, even in a child, for bone and flesh to grow perceptibly in anything less than weeks. Yet kneeling here now, the cold concrete pressing hard against my knees, I knew that the flesh I was staring at, and the bone underneath, had been re-forming themselves in only the hours and minutes that had so far passed of this night. It was simply not possible, but still I knew that these cheekbones had pushed up under this skin, the mouth had widened, the lips swelled and taken on character; that the chin had lengthened the fraction of an inch, the jaw angle altered, and I knew that the hair had changed in color to this precise shade, thickened and strengthened, twisting into waves, and begun to dip down onto the forehead.

I hope I never again in my life see anything as frightful as those eyes. I could look at them for only a second at a time, then I had to close my own. They were almost, but not quite — not yet — as large as Becky's. They were not quite the same shape, or precisely the same shade — but getting there. The *expression* of those eyes, though . . . Watch an unconscious person come to, and at first the eyes show only the least dull beginnings of comprehension, the first faint flickers of returning intelligence. That is all that had yet happened to these eyes. The steady awareness, the quiet alertness of Becky Driscoll's eyes were horribly parodied and diluted here. Yet, washed out a dozen times over as they were, you could nevertheless see, in these blank blue eyes caught in the trembling beam of my light, the first faint hint of what—given time—would become Becky Driscoll's eyes. I moaned, and bent double, clutching my stomach tight under my folded arms.

There was a scar on the left forearm of the thing on the shelf, just above the wrist. Becky had a small smooth burn mark there, and I remembered its shape because it crudely resembled an outline drawing of the South American continent. It was on this wrist, too, barely visible, but there, and precisely the same in shape. There was a mole on the left hip, and a pencil-line white scar just below the right kneecap; and although I didn't know it of my own knowledge, I was certain that Becky, too, was marked in these very same ways.

There on that shelf lay Becky Driscoll—uncompleted. There lay a . . . preliminary sketch for what was to become a perfect and flawless portrait, everything begun, all sketched in, nothing entirely finished. Or say it this way: there in that dim orange light lay a blurred face, seen vaguely, as through layers of water, and yet—recognizable in every least feature.

I jerked my head, tearing my eyes away, and sobbed for air—unconsciously I'd been holding my breath—and the sound was loud and harsh in that silent basement. Then I came to life once more, my heart swelling and contracting gigantically, the blood congesting in my veins and behind my eyes, in a panic of fright and excitement, and I got to my feet, my legs stiff, so that I stumbled.

Then I moved—fast—up the basement stairs and tried the first-floor door; it was unlocked, and I stepped out into the kitchen. On, then, through the silent dining room, the straight-backed chairs around the table silhouetted against the windows. In the living room I swung onto the white-railed staircase, turned at the landing, then climbed silently, two stairs at a time, to the upper hallway.

There was a row of doors, all closed, and I had to guess. I tried the second, on a hunch, grasping the knob, squeezing my fist tight around it, then slowly twisting my wrist, making no sound. I could feel, not hear, the latch sliding out of its notch in the door frame, then I pushed the door open through fractions of inches, and brought my head into the room, not moving my feet. A dark, formless blur, a head, lay on the single pillow of a double bed; there was no telling who it was. Aiming my light to one side of the face, I pressed the button, and saw Becky's father. He moved, muttering an unintelligible word, and I released my flash button and—fast, but still noiselessly—pulled the door closed, then gradually released my grip on the knob.

This was too slow. I couldn't contain myself; I was ready to burst through the doors, cracking them back against walls, ready to shout at the top of my lungs and rouse the household. I took two quick steps to the next door, opened it wide and strode in, my flashlight on and moving rapidly down the wall of the room to find the face of the sleeper in it. It was Becky, lying motionless in that little circle of light, the face a stronger, more vigorous duplicate of the parody of a face I'd left in the basement. I moved around the bed in two strides and grasped Becky's shoulder, my other hand holding the light. I shook, and she moaned a little but didn't waken, and now I got my arm under her shoulder and lifted. Her upper body came up to a sitting position, the head hanging back over my arm, and she sighed deep in her throat.

I didn't wait another second. Thrusting the little flash in my mouth, gripping it by the barrel in my teeth, I threw back the light blanket, got my other arm under her knees, and lifted. Then, staggering a step, I heaved Becky up over one shoulder in a fireman's carry. One arm curving up, holding her in place, I took the flash in my other hand, and staggered out into the hall. Then I walked, still staggering, but on tiptoe—I simply don't know how much or little sound I made—to the stairs, then down the stairway in the dark, sliding my feet, feeling for each step with my toes.

Out the front door, and then I was walking down the dark, empty street, alternately carrying Becky over my shoulder, then holding her, her head hanging limp, in my cradled arms. After a block she moaned, then lifted her head, eyes still closed, and her arms came up and clasped behind my neck. Then she opened her eyes.

For a moment, as I walked, looking down at her face, she stared at me, eyes drugged; then she blinked several times and her eyes cleared somewhat. Sleepily, like a child, she said, "What? What, Miles? What is it?"

"Tell you later," I said quietly, and smiled at her. "You're all right, I think. How do you feel?"

"All right. Tired, though. God, I'm tired." She was turning her head as she spoke, looking around her at the darkened houses, and the trees overhead. "Miles, what's *happening?*" She looked up at me, smiling puzzledly. "Are you kidnapping me? Carrying me off to your den, or something?" She looked down and saw that under my unbuttoned coat I was wearing pajamas. "Miles," she muttered mockingly, "couldn't you wait? Couldn't you at least ask me, like a gentleman? Miles, what in the *world* are you doing?"

I grinned at her. "I'll explain in a minute, when we get to my place." Her brows lifted at that, and my grin widened. "Don't worry, you're perfectly safe; Mannie Kaufman is there, and both the Belicecs."

Becky looked at me for a moment, then shivered suddenly; the night air was cool, and her nightgown was nylon. She tightened her grip around my neck and snuggled close, closing her eyes. "Too bad," she murmured. "The biggest adventure of my life: kidnapped from my bed, by a good-looking man in pajamas. Carried through the streets, like a captive cavewoman. And then he has to supply chaperons." She opened her eyes, and grinned up at me.

My arms ached horribly, my back felt as though a huge dull knife were pressing hard across my spine, and I could hardly straighten my knees after each step; it was agony. And yet I didn't want it to end; Becky felt good in my arms, close against me, and I was very aware of the pattern of warmth wherever her body touched mine.

Mannie was at my place, I saw; his car was parked back of mine. On the porch I set Becky on her feet, wondering if I could possibly straighten up without shattering into pieces like a broken glass. Then I gave her my topcoat, as I should have long since; I just hadn't thought. She put it on and buttoned it, smiling; then we walked in, and Mannie and Jack were in the living room.

They stared, mouths open, and Becky just smiled and greeted them, as though she were dropping in for tea. I acted equally casual, delighted at the looks on Jack's and Mannie's faces, and suggested to Becky that it was a little cool for a nightgown. I told her where she could find a clean pair of blue jeans that had shrunk and were too small for me, a clean white shirt, wool socks, and a pair of loafers, and she nodded, and went upstairs to find them.

I turned into the living room, toward an empty chair, glancing at Mannie and Jack. "It's just that I get lonesome sometimes," I said, and shrugged. "And when that happens, I've simply got to have company."

Mannie looked at me wearily. "Same thing?" he said quietly, nodding toward the stairs Becky had just climbed. "You find one at her place?"

"Yeah." I nodded, serious again. "In the basement."

"Well"—he stood up—"I want to see them. One of them, anyway. At her place, or Jack's."

I nodded. "Okay. Better make it Jack's; Becky's dad is at her place. I'll get some clothes on."

Upstairs, me in my bedroom, Becky in the bathroom a step or two down the hall, we each got dressed, and calling quietly to each other, were able to talk. Putting on pants, shoes and socks, a shirt, and my old blue sweater, I told her as briefly as possible what she had already guessed, what had happened at the Belicecs' and what I'd found in her basement, too, without going into details too much.

I was afraid of how it might affect her, but she took it okay. Both dressed now, we walked out into the hall, and Becky smiled at me pleasantly. She looked fine; the pants fitted pretty good, and with the white wool socks and loafers, her shirt sleeves rolled up, and the collar open, she looked like a girl in an ad for a vacation resort. Her eyes, I noticed now, were alive and eager, unafraid, and I realized that because she hadn't actually seen what I had, she was more pleased and delighted than anything else at all the excitement. "We're going to Jack's," I said. "Do you want to come?" I was ready to argue, if she did.

But she shook her head. "No, someone has to stay with Theodora. You all go ahead." She turned, walked into the room where Theodora lay, and I went on downstairs.

We took my car, all of us in the front seat, and after a few blocks, Jack said, "What do you think, Mannie?"

But Mannie just shook his head, staring absently at the dash. "I don't know yet," he said. "I just don't know." In the east, I noticed, though it was still black night in the car and the street around us, there was a hint of dawn or false dawn in the sky.

We climbed the dirt road in low gear, rounded the last turn, and every single light in Jack's house, it seemed, was blazing. For an instant it scared me—I expected the house to be utterly dark—and I had a quick mental image of a half-alive, naked, and staring figure stumbling vacant-mindedly through that house clicking on light switches. Then I realized that Jack and Theodora wouldn't have bothered turning off the lights when they'd left, and I calmed down a little. I parked outside the open garage, and in just the time it had taken to drive up here from my house, the sky had definitely lightened; all around us now you could see the black outlines of trees against the whitening light. We got out, and in a little circle at my feet I could see the irregularities of ground and the first grayed beginnings of color in the weeds and bushes. The lights of the house were beginning to go weak and orange in the wan light of first dawn.

None of us speaking a word, we walked single-file into the garage, Jack leading, the leather of our soles gritting on the cement floor. Then we were in the basement, the half-open door of the billiard room six or eight paces ahead. The light was on, just as Theodora had left it, and now Jack was pushing the door open.

He stopped so suddenly that Mannie bumped into him; then he moved slowly forward again, and Mannie and I filed in after him. There was no body on the table. Under the bright, shadowless light from overhead lay the brilliant green felt, and on the felt, except at the corners and along the sides, lay a sort of thick gray fluff that might have fallen, or been jarred loose, I supposed, from the open rafters.

For an instant, his mouth hanging open, Jack stared at the table. Then he swung to Mannie, and his voice protesting, asking for belief, he said, "It was there, on the table! Mannie, it *was!*"

Mannie smiled, nodding quickly. "I believe you, Jack; you all saw it." He shrugged. "And now someone's taken it. There's a mystery here, of some sort. Maybe. Come on, let's get outside; I think I've got something to tell you."

CHAPTER
SEVEN

A t the edge of the road in front of Jack's house, we sat down in the grass beside my car, our feet over the embankment, staring down at the town in the valley. I'd seen it like this more than once, coming through the hills from night-time calls. The roof tops were still gray and colorless, but all over the town now, windows flashed a dull blind orange in the almost level rays of the rising sun. Even as we watched, the orange-colored windows were brightening, lightening in tone, as the sun's rim moved, inching up over the eastern horizon. Here and there, from an occasional chimney, we could see a beginning straggle of smoke.

Jack murmured, speaking to himself actually, shaking his head, as he stared down at the toy houses below. "It just won't bear thinking about," he said. "How many of those things are down there in town right now? Hidden away in secret places."

Mannie smiled. "None," he said, "none at all," and
grinned as our heads swung to stare at him. "Listen,"
he said quietly, "you've got a mystery on your hands,
all right, and a real one. Whose body was that? And
where is it now?" We were seated at his left, and Mannie turned his head to watch our faces for a moment,
then he added, "But it's a completely normal mystery.
A murder, possibly; I couldn't say. Whatever it is,
though, it's well within the bounds of human experience; don't try to make any more of it."

My mouth opened to protest, but Mannie shook his
head. "Now listen to me," he said quietly. His forearms
on his knees, hands clasped, Mannie sat staring down
at the town. "The human mind is a strange and wonderful thing," he said reflectively, "but I'm not sure it
will ever figure itself out. Everything else, maybe—
from sub-atomic particles to the universe—except itself."

His arm swung outward, gesturing at the miniature
town below us, brightening in the first morning sun.
"Down there in Mill Valley a week or ten days ago,
someone formed a delusion; a member of his family was
not what he seemed, but an impostor. It's not a common
delusion precisely, but it happens occasionally, and
every psychiatrist encounters it sooner or later. Usually
he has some idea of how to treat it."

Mannie leaned back against the front wheel of my
car and smiled at us. "But last week I was stumped. It's
not a common delusion, yet from this one town alone
there were a dozen or more such cases, all occurring
within the past week or so. I'd never encountered such
a thing in all my practice before, and it had me stopped
cold." Mannie moved a hand absently over the stubble
of his dark tanned face. "But I've been doing some
reading lately, refreshing my mind on certain things I

should have remembered before. Did you ever hear of the Mattoon Maniac?"

We just shook our heads and waited.

"Well"—Mannie clasped one knee between his interlocked fingers—"Mattoon is a town in Illinois, of maybe twenty thousand people, and something happened there that you can find described in textbooks on psychology.

"On September 2, 1944, in the middle of the night, a woman phoned the police; someone had tried to kill her neighbor with poison gas. This neighbor, a woman, had awakened around midnight; her husband was at work on the night shift of a factory. The woman's room was filled with a peculiar, sweet-smelling, sickening odor. She tried to get up, but her legs were paralyzed. She managed to crawl to the phone and call her neighbor, who notified the police.

"The police arrived, and did what they could; they found a door unlocked, by which someone could have entered, but of course there was no one else around the house any more. A night or so later, the police got another call, and again found a partly paralyzed, very sick woman; someone had tried to kill her with poison gas. That same night, the same thing happened again, in another part of town. And when a dozen or more women were attacked in the same way on following nights, each sick and partly paralyzed from a sickly-smelling gas pumped into their rooms while they slept, the police knew they had a psychopath to find; a maniac, as the newspapers were calling him."

Mannie plucked a weed, and began stripping the leaves from the stem. "One night a woman saw the man. She awoke to see him silhouetted against her open bedroom window, and he was pumping something like an insecticide spray into her room. She got a whiff of the gas, screamed, and the man ran. But as he turned from the window, she got a good look at him; he was tall, quite thin, and was wearing what looked like a black skullcap.

"Now the State Police were called in, because in only a single night, seven more women were gassed and partly paralyzed. Reporters were in town too, from the press services, and most of the Chicago newspapers; you can find accounts of all this in their files. At night now, in Mattoon, Illinois, in 1944, cars filled with men carrying shotguns patrolled the streets; neighbors organized into squads, patrolling their own blocks in shifts; and the attacks continued, and the maniac wasn't found.

"Finally, one night, there were eight state police cars in town, and a mobile radio unit. A doctor, prepared and waiting, was at the local Methodist hospital. That night, the police got a call, as usual; a woman, hardly able to speak, had been gassed by the madman. In less than a minute, one of the roving police cars was at her house; she was rushed to the hospital and examined by the doctor." Mannie smiled. "He found absolutely nothing wrong with her; nothing. She was sent home, another call came in, and the second woman was rushed to the hospital, examined, and again there was nothing wrong with her. All night long that happened. The calls came in, the women were examined at the hospital within minutes, and every single one of them was sent back home."

For a long moment Mannie studied our faces, then he said, "The cases that night were the last that ever happened in Mattoon; the epidemic was over. There was no maniac; there never had been one." He shook his head in puzzlement. "Mass hysteria, auto-suggestion, whatever you want to call it—that's what happened to Mattoon. Why? How?" Mannie shrugged. "I don't know. We give it names, but we don't really understand it. All we know for sure is that these things actually happen."

I think Mannie saw, in my face and Jack's, a sort of stubborn unwillingness to accept the implications of what he was saying, because he turned to me and, voice patient, said, "Miles, you must have read, in med school, about the Dancing Sickness that spread over Europe a couple hundred years ago." He looked at Jack. "An astounding thing," he said. "Impossible to believe, except that it happened. Whole towns began to dance: first one person, then another, then every man, woman, and child in it, till they fell dead or exhausted. The thing swept all Europe; the Dancing Sickness; you can read about it in your encyclopedia. It lasted an entire summer, as I recall, and then—it stopped; died out. Leaving people, I suppose, wondering what in the world had happened to them." Mannie paused, watching us, then shrugged. "So there you are. These things are hard to believe till you see them, and even when you do see them.

"And that's what's happened in Mill Valley"—he nodded at the town at our feet. "The news spreads, semisecretly at first. It's whispered around, as it was in Mattoon; someone believes her husband, sister, aunt, or uncle is actually an undetectable impostor, a strange and exciting bit of news to hear. And then—it keeps on happening. And it spreads, and there's a new case, or several, nearly every day. Hell, the Salem witch hunt, UFO's—they're all part of this same amazing aspect of the human mind. People live lonely lives, a lot of them; these delusions bring attention and concern."

But Jack was slowly shaking his head no, and Mannie said quietly, "The body was real; that's what's bothering you, isn't it, Jack?" Jack nodded, and Mannie said, "Yes, it was; you all saw it. But that's all that's real. Jack, if you'd found that body a month ago, you'd have recognized it for what it was, a puzzling, possibly very strange mystery, but a perfectly natural one, too. And so would Theodora, Becky, and Miles. You can see what I mean." Leaning across me, he was staring at Jack intently. "Suppose that in August 1944, in Mattoon, Illinois, a man had walked through the streets at night carrying a spray gun. Anyone seeing him would have supposed, and correctly, that the man was going to spray his rose bushes next day, or something of the sort. But one month later, in September, that man with the spray gun might have had his head blown off before he ever had a chance to explain."

Gently, Mannie said, "And you, Jack, you found a body, of approximately your height and build, which isn't too strange; you're an average-sized man. The face, in death, and this happens often, was smooth and unlined, bland in expression, and"—Mannie shrugged —"well, you're a writer, an imaginative man, and you're under the influence of the delusion that's loose in Mill Valley, and so are Miles, Theodora, and Becky. Me, too, undoubtedly, if I lived here. And your mind leaped for a connection, leaped to a conclusion explaining two mysteries in terms of each other. The human mind searches for cause and effect, always; and we all prefer the weird and thrilling to the dull and commonplace as an answer."

"Listen, Mannie, Theodora actually *saw*—"

"Exactly what she *expected* to see! What she was frightened to death of seeing! What she was absolutely *certain* to see, under the circumstances. I'd really be astonished if she hadn't! Why, you two had her, and she had herself, completely conditioned and ready for it."

I started to speak, and Mannie grinned at me mockingly. "You saw nothing, Miles." He shrugged. "Except a rolled-up rug, maybe, on a shelf in Becky's basement. Or a pile of sheets or laundry; almost anything at all, or nothing at all, would do. You had yourself so worked up by then, Miles, so hyper-excited, running through the streets, that as you say yourself, you were certain you were going to find—what of course you did find. It was a lead-pipe cinch that you would." He held up a hand as I started to speak. "Oh, you saw it, all right. In every tiny detail. Exactly as you described it. You saw it as vividly and absolutely *real* as anyone has ever seen anything. But you saw it only in your mind." Mannie frowned at me. "Hell, you're a doctor, Miles; you know something about how this sort of thing works."

He was right; I did. In pre-med college, I once sat in a classroom listening to a psychology professor quietly lecturing, and now, sitting there on the edge of the road, the sun warming against my face, I was remembering how the door of that classroom had suddenly burst open, as two struggling men stumbled into the room. One man broke loose, yanked a banana from his pocket, pointed it at the other, and yelled, "Bang!" The other clutched his side, pulled a small American flag from his pocket, waved it violently in the other man's face, then they both rushed out of the room.

The professor said, "This is a controlled experiment. You will each take paper and pencil, write down a complete account of what you just saw, and place it on my desk as you leave the room."

Next day, in class, he read our papers aloud. There were some twenty-odd students, and no two accounts were alike, or even close. Some students saw three men, some four, and one girl saw five. Some saw white men, some blacks, some Orientals, some saw women. One student saw a man stabbed, saw the blood spurt, saw him hold a handkerchief to his side which quickly became blood-soaked, and could hardly believe it when he found no bloodstains on the floor, as he left his paper at the professor's desk. And so on, and so on. Not a single paper mentioned the American flag or the banana; those objects didn't fit into the sudden violent little scene that had burst on our senses, so our minds excluded them, simply ruled them out and substituted other more appropriate things such as guns, knives, and blood-soaked rags that we were each of us absolutely certain we'd seen. We *had* seen them, in fact; but only in our minds, hunting for some explanation.

So now I wondered if Mannie weren't right, and it was strange; I felt a sense of disappointment, a real let-down at the thought, and realized that I was trying to resist believing him. We do prefer the weird and thrilling, as Mannie had said, to the dull and commonplace. Even though I could still see in my mind, vivid and horribly real, what I'd thought I'd seen in Becky's basement, I felt, intellectually, that Mannie was probably right. But emotionally it was still very nearly impossible to accept, and I guess it showed in my face, and in Jack's.

Because Mannie got to his feet, and stood there for several seconds, looking down at us. Then he said, softly, "You want proof? I'll give it to you. Miles, go back to Becky's house and, in a calm state of mind, you'll see no body on that shelf in her basement; I guarantee that. There was only one body, in Jack's basement; the one that started all this. You want more proof? I'll give it to you. This delusion will die down in Mill Valley, just as it did in Mattoon, just as it did in Europe, just as all of them always do. And the people who came to you, Miles—Wilma Lentz and the others —will come back; some of them, anyway. Others will avoid you out of simple embarrassment. But if you hunt them up, they'll admit what the others tell you: that the delusion is gone, that they simply don't understand how or why it ever entered their heads. And that'll be the end of it; there'll be no more cases. I guarantee you that, too."

Mannie grinned then, glanced around him at the sky, blue and clear now, and said, "I could use some breakfast." Jack smiled up at him, getting to his feet, and so did I. "Me, too," I answered. "Come on back to my place, and let's see what the ladies can find us to eat." Jack went through his house, then, turning off lights, closing and locking doors. When he came out, he had a brown cardboard folder under his arm, the accordion type, divided into sections, every one of them crammed to bulging with papers. "My office," he said, nodding down at the folder. "Work-in-progress, notes, references, junk. Very valuable stuff"—he grinned—"and I like to keep it with me." Then we all drove back down the hill to town.

At Becky's house I stopped at the curb, and got out, leaving the motor running. It was still very early, the street white with new daylight, and I didn't see a soul or movement in the entire block. I walked boldly around to the side of the house, but on the grass, my feet making no sound. At the broken basement window I stood glancing up at the neighbors' windows; I didn't see anyone, or hear a sound. I stooped quickly, crawled in through the window, then walked across the concrete floor on tiptoes. The basement was light, now, and very silent, and I was calm but worried; I didn't want to be caught down there and have to explain what I was doing.

The cupboard door I'd opened stood half ajar as I'd left it, and now I opened it wide and lowered my eyes to the bottom shelf. The light from a nearby basement window struck it full, and the shelf was empty. I opened every door in that wall of shelves, and there was nothing that didn't belong there; only canned goods, tools, empty fruit jars, old newspapers. On the empty bottom shelf lay a thick mass of gray fluff and, squatting beside it, I shrugged; it was the kind of dust and dirt, I could only suppose, that accumulates in basements, and which my senses had distorted, in a kind of hysterical explosion, into a body.

I didn't want to stay a moment longer than I had to, and I closed the cupboard, as I'd found it, crossed to the window, and crawled out onto the side lawn again. What Becky's father would think of this broken window when he found it, I didn't know; but I knew I wasn't going to explain it.

In the car, drawing away from the curb, I nodded at Mannie, grinning a little sheepishly. "You were right," I said, and I glanced at Jack and shrugged.

CHAPTER
EIGHT

The human animal won't take a straight diet of any emotion: fear, happiness, horror, grief, or even contentment. It was queer; after the night we'd all spent, breakfast was fun. The sun helped; it streamed in through the open windows and the kitchen door, yellow and warm and full of morning promise. Theodora was up when we got there, sitting at the kitchen table drinking coffee with Becky. She stood up as we came in, Jack hurrying toward her, and then they held each other tight for a long moment, Jack kissing her hard. He drew back to look at her then, and Mannie and I looked, too. She was still tired, there were circles under her eyes, but the eyes were calm and sane now, and she smiled at us over Jack's shoulder.

Then, almost as though a signal had been given, we all began chattering, laughing a lot, making jokes; and the two women began turning on gas jets, getting out skillets and pans, opening cupboards and the refrigerator, while we three men sat down at the kitchen table. Becky poured us each some coffee. By a sort of unspoken consent, we didn't talk about the night before—not seriously, anyway—or about what Jack, Mannie, and I had just been doing, and the women asked no questions; they must have felt from our manner that things were all right.

Sausage began sputtering on the stove, Theodora turning it with a fork, and Becky began beating up eggs in a bowl, the metal spoon tapping rhythmically against the china, a nice sound. Theodora said, eyes laughing, "I've been thinking it over, and I could use a duplicate of Jack. One of them could moon around the house as usual, not hearing a word I say, working out whatever he's writing in his mind. And maybe the other would have time to talk to me, and even help with the dishes once in a while."

Jack smiled at her over the rim of his cup, his eyes happy and relieved to see her this way. "Might be worth trying," he said. "At times I think any change in me would be an improvement. Maybe the new one would actually know how to write, instead of beating his head against a stone wall just trying."

Becky was nodding. "There are advantages, all right," she said. "I like the idea of one me secretly carried through the streets in her nightgown, while the other is still home, properly alone in her bed, satisfying all the proprieties."

We rang the changes on that idea. Mannie wanted one Dr. Kaufman listening to his patients, while the other was out playing tennis, and I said I could use a duplicate Miles Bennell to catch up on sleep.

The food tasted wonderful, and we ate and chattered all through breakfast, making what jokes there were to be made. Actually, I think, we were a little too lively, almost high, in reaction against what had happened. Presently Mannie touched his mouth with his napkin, glanced at the wall clock, and stood up. By the time he got home, he said, and shaved, changed clothes, and got to his office, he'd just have time to keep his first appointment. He said his good-byes, told me he planned to send me an enormous bill, charging his usual hourly rates, if not double, grinned, and I saw him to the front door. Then the rest of us all had second or third cups of coffee.

While I sipped mine, I sat back in my chair, and told Theodora and Becky, briefly and factually, what had happened, what we'd found—or rather, hadn't found—in Jack's and Becky's basements, and what Mannie had told us, there on the road in front of Jack's house.

I expected what happened when I finished; Theodora simply shook her head, her lips compressed in quiet stubbornness. It just wasn't possible for her to believe that she hadn't seen what she was certain she had seen—and could still see in her mind's eye. Becky didn't comment, but I could see from the relief in her eyes that she'd accepted Mannie's explanation, and I knew she was thinking of her father. She looked very good, sitting there at the table beside me, very fresh and alive and good-looking, and it was exciting to see her wearing my shirt, open at the collar.

Jack got up, walked to the living room, and came back with the cardboard folder he'd brought from his house. Smiling, he sat down, saying, "I'm kind of a squirrel," and began peering into each section of the accordion-folder. "A collector of various things, without quite knowing why. And one of the things I save"—he reached into one section of his folder, and brought out a great handful of newspaper clippings—"are certain newspaper items. I brought them along, after we talked to Mannie." Pushing aside the plates before him, he put the clippings on the table, a mound of dozens of them, some yellowing a little with age, some new-looking, most of them short, a few of them long. Picking one from the pile at random, he glanced at the heading, then passed it over to me.

I held it so Becky could read, too. *Frogs Fell on Alabama,* the heading said. It was a little one-column story, a couple inches long, date-lined, *Edgeville, Ala:* "Any fishermen in this town of four thousand," it began, "had plenty of bait this morning—if there was only a place in this area to use it. Last night a shower of tiny frogs, of undetermined origin..." The little story —I skimmed through the rest of it—went on to say that a shower of small frogs had fallen on the town, pelting the roofs and windows like rain, for several minutes the previous night. The tone of the story was mildly humorous, and no explanation of the shower was given.

I looked up at Jack, and he smiled. "Silly, isn't it?" he said. "Especially since, as the story itself suggests, there was no place the frogs could have come from." He picked up another clipping and handed it to me.

Man Burned to Death; Clothes Unharmed this was headed, and it said that a man had been found burned to a cinder, in an Idaho farmhouse. The clothes he wore, however, weren't burned or even singed, and there wasn't a sign of fire damage or even smoke smudges in the house. The local coroner was quoted as saying it would take heat of at least 2000 degrees to burn a man as this one had been found. That's all the story said.

I half smiled, half frowned at Jack, wondering what this was all about. Theodora was looking at him over the rim of her coffee cup with the wryly amused look of affectionate scorn wives have for their husbands' eccentricities, and Jack grinned at us. "I've got a couple dozen like that, from all over—people burned to death inside their clothes. Ever read such nonsense in your life? Here's another kind."

Written in pencil on the margin of this one was, *New Yk. Post,* and the printed heading said, *And There Was His Ambulance.* The date line was *Richmond, Cal., May 7 (AP).* The clipping read: "'Hurry to San Pablo and MacDonald Ave.,' said the telephone voice. 'The Santa Fe streamliner just hit a truck and a man is hurt pretty badly.' Police dispatched a squad car and ambulance to the address. There was no accident. The train hadn't yet reached the scene. It did, though, just as the investigators were leaving, and just as a delivery truck driven by Randolph Bruce, 44, was on the crossing. Bruce is hurt pretty badly. He has a brain injury and a crushed chest."

I laid down the clipping. "What's your point, Jack?"

"Well"—he got slowly to his feet—"there are a couple hundred queer little happenings that I've collected in just a few years; and you could find thousands more." He began slowly pacing the kitchen floor. "I think they prove at least this; that strange things happen, really do *happen,* every now and then, here and there throughout the world. Things that simply don't fit in with the great body of knowledge that the human race has gradually acquired over thousands of years. Things in direct contradiction to what we know to be true. Something falls up, instead of down."

Reaching out to the toaster on the drainboard of the sink, Jack touched a finger tip to a crumb, and lifted it to his tongue. "So this is my point, Miles.

Should they always be explained away? Or laughed away? Or simply ignored? Because that's what always happens." He resumed his slow pacing about the big old kitchen. "I guess it's only natural. I suppose nothing can be given a place in our body of accepted knowledge, except what is universally experienced. Science claims to be objective, though." He stopped, facing the table. "To consider all phenomena impartially and without prejudice. But of course it does no such thing. This kind of occurrence"—he nodded at the little mound of paper on the table—"it dismisses with automatic habitual contempt. From which the rest of us take our cue. What are these things, say the scientific attitude? Why, they're only optical illusions, or self-suggestion, or hysteria, or mass hypnosis, or when everything else fails—coincidence. Anything and everything, except that possibly they really happened. Oh, no"—Jack shook his head smiling—"you must never admit for a moment that anything we don't understand may nevertheless have occurred."

As I believe most wives, even the wisest, do with any real conviction held by their husbands, Theodora accepted this and made it her own. "Well, it's stupid," she said, "and how the human race ever learns anything new, I really don't know."

"It takes a long time," Jack agreed. "Hundreds of years to accept the fact that the world is round. A century resisting the knowledge that the earth revolves around the sun. We hate facing new facts or evidence, because we might have to revise our conceptions of what's possible, and that's always uncomfortable."

Jack grinned, and sat down at the table again. "I should talk, though. Take any of these." He picked up a clipping. "This one from the *New York Post*, for example. Now, that isn't fiction. The *New York Post* is a real newspaper, and this little story was actually printed in the *Post* and no doubt in a lot of other papers all over the country. Thousands read it, including me. But did we rise up insisting that our body of knowledge be revised to include this strange little occurrence? Did *I?* No; we wondered about it, were intrigued and interested momentarily, then dismissed it from mind. And now, like all the other odd little happenings that don't quite fit in with what we think we know, it's forgotten and ignored by the world, except for a few curiosa collectors like me."

"Maybe it should be," I said quietly. "Take a look at this." I'd been idly glancing through his clippings as Jack talked, and now I pushed one toward him. It was just a squib from *The Mill Valley Record*, and it didn't say much. One L. Bernard Budlong, botany and biology professor at Marin College, was quoted as denying a comment the paper had attributed to him the day before, about some "mysterious objects" found on some pasture land outside of town. They were described as large seed pods of some sort or other, and now Budlong was denying having said that they'd "come from outer space." The *Record* apologized: "Sorry, Prof!" the story ended.

"What about that, Jack?" I said gently. "The collapse of one of your little items: a one-inch retraction buried in the paper a day or so later. Makes you wonder"—I nodded at his mound of clippings—"about all the rest, doesn't it?"

"Sure," Jack said. "That retraction belongs in the collection, too. And that's why it's there; I didn't exclude it." He picked up a handful of clippings and let them flutter down onto the table again. "Miles, these are *lies*, most of them, for all I know. Some are most certainly hoaxes. And maybe most of the rest are distortions, exaggerations, or simple errors of judgment or vision; I have sense enough to know that. But, damn it, Miles, not all of them, past, present, and future! You can't explain them *all* away, perpetually and forever!"

For a moment he sat glaring at me, then he smiled. "So is Mannie right? Should what happened last night be explained away, too?" Jack shrugged. "Maybe it should. Mannie makes good sense; he always does. And he's explained what happened *almost satisfactorily*; maybe ninety-nine percent." For a moment Jack stared at us, then lowered his voice, and said very softly, "But there's a tiny one percent of doubt still left in my mind."

I was looking at Jack, and feeling an actual, unpleasant, sluggish prickling along my spine at the simple thought that had just occurred to me. "The fingerprints," I murmured, and Jack frowned momentarily. "The blank fingerprints!" I shouted then. "Mannie thinks it's just an ordinary body. Since when do ordinary men have no fingerprints at all!"

Theodora was pushing herself up from her chair, arms straining against the table top, and her voice came out high and shrill. "I can't go *back* there, Jack! *I can't set foot in that house!*" Her voice, as Jack stumbled to his feet, rose still higher. "I *know* what I saw; it was turning into *you*. Jack, it *was!*" And as he took her into his arms, the tears were tumbling down her cheeks, and the fear stood in her eyes again.

After a moment I was able to speak quietly. "Then don't go," I said to Theodora. "Stay right here." They both turned to look at me, and I said, "You've got to, both of you." I smiled a little. "It's a big house; pick out a room and stay; bring your typewriter down, Jack, and work. I'd love to have you. I rattle around in this house, and I could use some company."

Jack studied my face for a moment. "You sure?"

"Absolutely."

He looked down at Theodora, and she nodded dumbly, pleadingly. "All right," Jack said to me then. "Maybe we'd better; for a day or so. Thanks, Miles, thanks a lot."

"You, too, Becky," I said then. "You've got to stay, too—for a few days, anyway. With Theodora and Jack," something made me add.

Her face was pale, but she grinned a little at that. "With Theodora and Jack," she repeated. "And where'll you be?"

My face flushed, but I smiled. "Right here," I agreed, "but you can ignore me."

Theodora looked up from Jack's shoulder, and now she was able to smile, too. "It might be fun, Becky," she said.

Becky's eyes were dancing. "It might at that, a sort of house party that goes on for days." Then the fear came into her eyes again. "I was just thinking of my dad, is all," she said to me.

"Phone him," I said, "and just tell him the truth. That something has upset Theodora pretty badly, she's going to stay here, and she needs you. That's all you have to say." I grinned. "Though you might add that I have some plans in mind that you can't resist." I glanced at the wall clock. "I've got to get to work, kids; the place is yours." Then I went upstairs to get ready for the office.

I was more irritated than scared, standing at my bathroom mirror, shaving. A part of my mind was frightened at the fact we'd just faced downstairs: that the body in Jack's basement, incredibly, impossibly, and undeniably, had had no fingerprints. We hadn't imagined that, I knew, and it was a fact Mannie's explanation couldn't cover. But mostly, leaning toward the mirror scraping my face, I was annoyed; I didn't *want* Becky Driscoll living here in my house, where I'd see her more every day than I ordinarily would in a week. She was too attractive, likable, and good-looking.

I talk to myself when I shave. "You handsome bastard," I said to my face. "You can marry them, all right; you just can't stay married, that's your trouble. You are weak. Emotionally unstable. Basically insecure. A latent thumb-sucker. A cesspool of immaturity, unfit for adult responsibility." I smiled, and tried to think of some more. "You are undoubtedly a quack, and a Don Juan personality. A pseudo—" I cut it out, and finished shaving with the uncomfortable feeling that for all I knew it wasn't funny but true, that having failed with one woman, I was getting too involved with another, and that for my sake and hers, she should be anywhere but here under my roof.

Jack rode downtown with me to talk to Nick Grivett, the local police chief; we both knew him well. Jack had, after all, found a dead body; and it had disappeared. He had to report that. But we decided, on the way down in my car, that he'd report just those bare facts, nothing more. We couldn't explain his delay in reporting, so we decided he'd alter the time sequence a little, and say he found the body last night, instead of the morning before; it might just as well have happened that way.

Even at that, there'd be a little delay to account for; why hadn't he phoned the police last night, then? We decided Jack would explain that Theodora was upset and hysterical; he couldn't think of anything else till she was taken care of, and had rushed her to a doctor, me. She'd had a bad shock, so they were staying at my place, and Jack had gone home to pick up some clothes before phoning the police; and then he'd discovered the body was gone. We figured Grivett would bawl him out a little, but there wasn't much else he could do. Smiling, I told Jack to act as dopey and absentminded as he could, and Grivett would put it all down to his being an impractical literary type.

Jack nodded and smiled a little at that, then his face went serious again. "Forget the fingerprints, too, you think? When I talk to Grivett?"

I shrugged and grimaced. "You'll have to. Grivett would have you committed if you mentioned that." We'd pulled up at the police station, Jack got out, and I grinned and waved then; and drove on.

CHAPTER

NINE

But I was in a bad mood when I parked my car—on a side street near my office, just out of the parking-meter zone. Worry, doubt, and fear were twisting through my mind as I walked the block and a half to the office, and the look of Throckmorton Street depressed me. It seemed littered and shabby in the morning sun, a city trash basket stood heaped and unemptied from the day before, the globe of an overhead street light was broken, and a few doors from the building where my office was, a shop stood empty. The windows were whitened, and a clumsily painted *For Rent* sign stood leaning against the glass. It didn't say where to apply, though, and I had the feeling no one cared whether the store was ever rented again. A smashed wine bottle lay in the entranceway of my building, and the brass nameplate set in the gray stone of the building was mottled and unpolished. All up and down the street, as I stopped for a moment to look, not a soul was out washing down a store window as the shop-owners usually were of a morning, and the street seemed oddly deserted. It was simply the mood I was in, I told myself; I was looking at the world in fear and worry, and I reprimanded myself; it's no way to let yourself feel when you're diagnosing and treating patients.

A patient was waiting when I got upstairs; she had no appointment, but I was a little early, so I worked her in. She was Mrs. Seeley, the quiet little woman of forty who had sat in this same chair a week before telling me that her husband wasn't her husband at all. Now she was smiling, actually squirming with relief and pleasure, as she told me her delusion was gone. She'd talked to Dr. Kaufman last week as I'd suggested, she told me; he hadn't seemed to help her much, but last evening, unexplainedly, she'd "come to her senses."

"I was sitting in the living room reading," she said eagerly, clasping her hands nervously on her purse, "when suddenly I looked up at Al across the room; he was watching television." She shook her head in happy bewilderment. "And I knew it was him. Really him, I mean—Al, my husband. Dr. Bennell"—she stared at me wonderingly across the desk—"I just don't know what happened last week; I really don't know, and I feel so foolish. Of course"—she sat back in her chair—"I had heard of another case like mine. A lady in my club told me about it; said there'd been several such cases in town. And Dr. Kaufman explained to me that hearing about those cases . . ."

When she'd told me, finally, what Dr. Kaufman had said, and what she had said, and I'd listened, and nodded, and smiled, I got her out of the office—still talking—in a fairly reasonable time. She'd have stayed all afternoon, bubbling over, if I'd let her.

My nurse had come in while Mrs. Seeley was talking, and brought in my appointment list. I glanced down it, now, and—sure enough—there was the name of one of the three mothers of high-school girls who had called on me so frantically the week before. She was down for three-thirty, and later that afternoon, when my nurse ushered her in, she was smiling, and before she even sat down, began telling me what I knew I'd hear. The girls were all right, and fonder than ever of their English instructor. The teacher had accepted their apologies gracefully, showing some understanding of what had happened; and she'd made the sensible suggestion that the girls simply explain to their schoolmates that it had all been a joke, a school-girl hoax. They'd done this, and successfully. Their friends, the mother in my office assured me, actually admired the girls' skill as pranksters, and now she, the mother, wasn't worried a bit. Dr. Kaufman had explained to her how easily such a delusion can affect a person, particularly adolescent girls.

The moment the happy mother had left, I picked up my phone, called Wilma Lentz at her shop, and when she answered, I asked her casually how she was feeling these days. There was a pause before she replied, then she said, "I've been meaning to stop in and see you about—what happened." She laughed, not very successfully, then said, "Mannie helped me, all right, Miles, just the way you said. The delusion, or whatever it was, is gone, and—Miles, I've been so embarrassed. I don't quite know what happened, or how in the world to explain to you, but—"

I interrupted to tell her I understood what had happened, that she wasn't to worry or feel badly, but to just forget it, and that I'd be seeing her.

I sat there for maybe a full minute after I hung up,

my hand still on the phone, trying to think coolly and sensibly. Everything Mannie had predicted had come true. And—the temptation to believe was very strong —if he was right about all that had happened, I could simply let the fear in my mind fade away, now. And Becky could go home tonight.

Almost angrily, I asked myself this: was I going to let nothing more than the absence of fingerprints on that body in Jack's basement keep all my problems and fears alive and unresolved? A picture rose up in my mind, and existed for a moment, sharp and clear; once more I could see those smudged fingerprints, horribly, impossibly, yet undeniably smooth as a baby's cheek. Then the clarity of that mental image broke and faded, and I told myself irritably that there were a dozen perfectly possible and natural explanations, if I wanted to bother taking the trouble to think of them.

I said it aloud. "Mannie is right. Mannie's explained—" *Mannie, Mannie, Mannie,* I thought to myself suddenly. That's all I seemed to be hearing and thinking lately. He'd explained our delusion last night, and now this morning every patient I talked to seemed to mention his name ecstatically and gratefully; he'd solved everything in no time, and single-handed. For a moment I thought of the Mannie Kaufman I'd always known, and it seemed to me he'd always been more cautious, slow to form final opinions. Then the notion roared up in my mind full-blown; this *wasn't* the Mannie I'd always known; it wasn't Mannie at all, but only looked, talked, and acted like—

I actually shook my head to clear it; then I smiled, a little ruefully. This in itself was more proof of how right he had been, fingerprints or not; proof of just what he'd explained—the incredible strength of the weird delusion that had swept Mill Valley. I lifted my hand from the telephone on my desk. The late-afternoon fall sunlight was slanting in through my office windows, and from the street below I heard all the little sounds of a normal world moving through its daily routine. And now what had happened last night lost its strength, in the routine activity, and bright sunlight all around me. Mentally tipping my hat to Mannie Kaufman, eminent shrink, I told myself—insisted to myself—that he was exactly what he'd always been, an extremely intelligent, perceptive guy. He was right, we'd acted foolishly and hysterically, and there wasn't a sensible reason why Becky Driscoll shouldn't be back home where she belonged tonight, in her own house and bed.

I pulled into my driveway around eight that evening, after my hospital calls, and I saw that they'd waited supper for me. It was still light, and Theodora and Becky were out on the porch, wearing aprons they'd found in the house somewhere, and setting out supper on the wide wooden porch rails. They waved at me, smiling, and upstairs from an open window, as I slammed the car door, I could hear Jack's typewriter, and the house seemed alive once again with people I liked, and I felt wonderful.

Jack came down, and we had supper on the porch. It had been a clear, blue-sky day, pretty warm for the time of year, but now—no longer full daylight—it was just exactly right. There was a tiny, very balmy breeze, and you could hear the leaves of the big old trees that lined the street stirring and sighing with pleasure. The birds chirped, and from down the block you could hear the far-off rackety clatter of a lawnmower, one of the best sounds there is. We sat there on the wide old porch in the comfortably battered wicker furniture, or the porch swing, eating bacon-and-tomato sandwiches on toast, sipping coffee, talking about nothing much, with frequent easy silences, and I knew this was one of those occasional wonderful moments you remember always.

Becky had gone home and gotten some clothes, apparently; she was wearing one of those smart, cool-looking thin dresses that turn good-looking women into beautiful ones, and I smiled at her; she was sitting near me on the swing. "Would you care to come upstairs," I said politely, "and be seduced?"

"Love to," she murmured, and took a sip of her coffee, "but I'm too hungry just now."

"So sweet," Theodora said. "Jack, why didn't you say nice things like that when you were courting me?"

"I didn't dare," he said, and took a bite of his sandwich, "or you'd have trapped me into marriage."

I felt my face flush at that, but it was dark enough so I was sure no one had noticed. I could have told them, now, what had happened today at my office; but if I had, Becky might have wanted to go home right away, and I told myself I at least deserved a date for the evening. There was no danger in that, since I'd be taking her home soon.

Presently Theodora finished, and stood up. "I'm dead," she said. "Exhausted. And I'm going to bed." She looked down at Jack. "How about you, Jack? I think you should," she added firmly.

He glanced up at her, then nodded. "Yeah," he said, "I guess I ought to." He swallowed the last of his coffee, tossed the dregs on the lawn, and got up from the porch rail. "See you in the morning," he said to Becky and me. "'Night."

I didn't say anything to stop them. Becky and I replied good night, and watched the Belicecs walk on into the house, then heard them walking toward the stairs, talking quietly. I wasn't sure whether Theodora was actually tired or just up to a little match-making—

it seemed to me she'd urged Jack to leave just a little pointedly. But whichever it was, I didn't care, and what I had to tell them could wait till morning. Because I was a little tired at the moment of being a monk, and now I told myself that I'd earned a little time alone with Becky; that I'd tell her after a while what had happened today at my office.

We heard footsteps reach the top landing, then I turned to Becky. "Would you mind moving? And sit at my left, instead of my right?"

"No." She stood up, smiling puzzledly. "But why?" She sat down on the swing again, at my left.

I leaned across her for a moment to set my cup on the porch rail. "Because"—I smiled at her—"I kiss left-handed, if you know what I mean."

"No, I don't." She smiled back.

"Well, a woman at my right"—I demonstrated, curving my arm around empty space at my right side—"is uncomfortable for me. It just doesn't feel right somehow; it's something like trying to write with the wrong hand. I just don't kiss well, except to my left."

I lifted an arm to the back of the swing then, touching her shoulders, and Becky smiled a little, and turned toward me. Then I held her to me, bending toward her a little, shifting my position a bit, getting my arms around her just right, till we were both comfortable. I wanted this kiss, very much. My heart was suddenly banging away, and I could feel the tightness of blood in my temples. I kissed Becky then, slowly and very gently, taking my time; then harder, tightening my arms around her, bending her backward, and suddenly it was more than pleasant, it was a silent explosion in my mind, and through every nerve and vein in my body. I felt her lips, soft and strong, felt my hands pressed hard on her back and side, and the terrible thrill of her body against me. My head yanked back—I couldn't breathe. Then I was kissing her again, and suddenly, instantly, I didn't care what happened. I'd never in my life experienced anything like this, and my hand dropped down, tight on her thigh, and I knew I was going to take this woman upstairs with me if I could.

"*Miles!*"... I heard the sound, a man's harsh whisper coming from I didn't know where; I couldn't seem to think. "*Miles!*" It came louder, and I was looking stupidly around the porch. "Over here, Miles, *quick!*" It was Jack, standing just inside the closed screen door, and now I saw him beckoning.

It was Theodora—I knew it—something had happened to her, and I was hurrying, crossing the porch, then following Jack across the living room toward the staircase. But Jack was walking on past the stairs into the hallway, then he was opening the basement door, and as he snapped on the flashlight in his hand, I walked down the stairs after him.

We crossed the basement, the leather of our soles gritting the hard dust on the floor; then Jack twisted the wood latch of the old coalbin door. The bin was in a corner of the basement, walled off from the rest of the room by ceiling-high planking, and it stood empty and unused now, washed out and hosed down since my father had installed gas heat long ago. Jack opened the door, and the beam of his flashlight moved across the floor, then steadied, an oval of light on the floor.

I couldn't get clear in my mind what I was seeing, lying there on the concrete. Staring, I had to describe to myself, a bit at a time, just what I was looking at, trying to puzzle out what it was. There lay, I finally decided, what looked like four giant seed pods. They had been round in shape, maybe three feet in diameter, and now they had burst open in places, and from the inside of the great pods, a grayish substance, a heavy fluff in appearance, had partly spilled out onto the floor.

That was a part of what I saw, my mind still busy trying to sort out impressions. In a way—at a glance— these giant pods reminded me of tumbleweed, those puffballs of dry, tangled vegetable matter, light as air, designed by nature to roll with the wind across the desert. But these pods were enclosed. I saw that their surfaces were made up of a network of tough-looking yellowish fibers, and stretching between these fibers, to completely enclose these pod-like balls, were great patches of brownish, dry-looking membrane, resembling a dead oak leaf in color and texture.

"Seed pods," Jack said softly, his voice astonished. "Miles . . . the seed pods in the clipping."

I just stared at him.

"The clipping you showed me this morning," he said impatiently, "quoting some college professor. It mentioned seed pods, Miles, giant seed pods, found somewhere west of town last summer." For a moment longer he stood staring at me, till I nodded. Then Jack pushed the coalbin door open wider, and in the moving, searching beam of his flashlight we saw something more, and stepped inside the bin to squat beside the things on the floor for a closer look. Each pod had burst open in four or five places, a part of the gray substance that filled them spilling out onto the floor. And now, in the closer beam of Jack's light, we saw a curious thing. At the outer edges, farthest away from the pods, the gray fluff was turning white, almost as though contact with the air was robbing it of color. And—there was no denying this; we could see it—the tangled fluffy substance was compressing itself, and achieving a form.

I once saw a doll made by a primitive South American people. It was made from flexible reeds, crudely plaited, and tied off in places, to form a head and body, arms and legs protruding stiffly from it. The tangled masses of what looked like grayish horsehair at our feet were slowly spilling out of the membranous pods, lightening in color at their outer edges, and—crudely but definitely—had begun forming themselves, the fibers straightening and aligning, into the rough approximation, each of them, of a head, a body, and miniature arms and legs. They were as crude as the doll I had seen—and just as unmistakable.

It's hard to say how long we squatted there, staring in stunned wonder at what we were seeing. But it was long enough to see the gray substance continue to exude, slowly as moving lava, from the great pods out onto the concrete floor. It was long enough to see the gray substance lighten and whiten after it reached the air. And it was long enough to see the crude head-and-limb-shaped masses grow in size as the gray stuff spilled out—and to become less crude.

We watched, motionless, our mouths open, and occasionally the brown membranous surfaces of the huge pods cracked audibly—the sound of a brittle leaf snapping in two—and the pods crumpled steadily, slowly collapsing a little at a time, as the lava-like flow of the substance they were filled with continued to flow out, like a heavy, infinitely slow-moving fog. And just as a motionless cloud in a windless sky imperceptibly changes in shape as you watch, the doll-like forms on the floor became—no longer dolls. They were, presently, as large as infants; and the pods that had held the substance forming them were crumbling to brittle fragments. The nearly motionless weaving and aligning of whitening fiber had continued; and now the heads were indented in a vague approximation of eye sockets, a ridge of a nose had formed on each, a crease of a mouth, and at the ends of the arms, bent now at the elbows, the starlike shapes of tiny, stiff-fingered hands were forming themselves.

Jack's head and mine turned together, and we stared into each other's eyes, knowing what, presently, we would see. "The blanks," he whispered, his voice rusty, "that's where they come from—they grow!"

We could no longer watch it. We stood suddenly, our legs stiff from crouching, and stumbled out into the basement, our eyes darting, frantically hunting normality. Then we stopped at nothing more than a pile of old newspapers, staring numbly down, in the light of Jack's flash, at the front page of an old *San Francisco Chronicle*, and the headlines and captions, the murder, violence, and corruption of a city, were understandable, and normal, and seemed almost good to see. We wandered the basement, slowly, saying nothing, pacing and waiting, thinking what stunned, confused thoughts we were able to. Then we walked back to the open coalbin door.

The impossible process inside was nearly finished. The great shattered pods lay on the floor now in tiny broken fragments, an almost unnoticeable dust. And where they had been, four figures now lay, large as adults, and the thick skeins of sticky fiber that composed them were united at all edges now, the surfaces unbroken, rough as corduroy still, but smoothing out steadily, and entirely white. Four blanks, the faces bland, smooth, and unmarked, lay almost ready to receive the final impressions. And they lay there, one for each of us, we knew: one for me, one for Jack, one each for Theodora and Becky. "Their weight," Jack murmured, fighting to hold on to sanity with words. "They absorb water from the air. The human body is eighty percent water. They absorb it; that's how it works."

Squatting beside the nearest, I lifted the hand to stare numbly at the smooth, rounded absence of fingerprints, and two thoughts filled my mind simultaneously: *They're going to get us*, I thought, lifting my head to stare at Jack, and at the same time—*Now, Becky has to stay here.*

CHAPTER
TEN

The time was 2:21 in the morning; I'd just glanced at my watch, and there were nine minutes to go before I woke Jack for his shift. I was patrolling the house, walking soundlessly along the upstairs hallway in my stocking feet; and now I stopped at the door of Becky's room. Noiselessly I opened it, walked in, and then, for the third time since midnight, I explored every inch of that room with my flashlight, just as I had every other room in the house. Stooping, I swept the beam under her bed; then I opened the closet and examined it.

Then, the beam of blue-white light focused on the wall just over Becky's head, I looked at her face. Her lips were slightly parted, her breathing regular, and her eyelashes curved down to lie on her cheek, a beautiful sight. She was very pretty, lying there, and I realized I was thinking how comforting it would be to be able to lie down beside her for a minute, to feel her stir sleepily, and feel the warmth of her next to me. Then I turned toward the hallway and the attic stairs.

There was nothing in the attic that didn't belong there. In the beam of my flashlight I saw the row of my mother's dresses and coats, suspended on hangers from a length of pipe, and covered with a sheet to keep off the dust; on the floor beside them was her old cedar chest. I saw my father's wooden filing cabinet, his framed diplomas stacked on top of it, just as they'd been brought from his office. In that cabinet lay records of the colds, cut fingers, cancers, broken bones, mumps, diphtheria, births and deaths of a large part of Mill Valley for over two generations. Half the patients listed in those files were dead now, the wounds and tissue my father had treated only dust.

I walked to the dormer window where I used to sit and read when I was a boy, and looked out at Mill Valley spreading away into the darkness below me. There they lay, the people of the town, sleeping out there in the dark; my father had brought a good many of them into the world. There was a night breeze stirring, and off to my left, on the pavement under the overhead street lamp, the fuzzy expanded shadows of the overhead telephone wires swung soundlessly back and forth over the deserted street, a lonely sight. I could see the McNeeleys' front porch, standing out sharply in the electric night-time glare of the street light, and the black shadowed bulk of their house behind it. I could see the Greesons' porch, too; I'd played house there with Dot Greeson when I was seven years old. Their long porch railing sagged inward in a shallow curve, and it needed painting, and I wondered why they'd let it go; they'd always kept up their place very neatly. Past the Greesons' I could make out the white picket fence around Blaine Smith's place; this town lying out there in the darkness was filled with neighbors and friends. I knew a lot of them, at least by sight, or to nod or speak to on the street. I'd grown up here; from boyhood I'd known every street, house, and path, most of the back yards, and every hill, field, and road for miles around.

And now I didn't know it any more. Unchanged to the eye, what I was seeing out there now—in my eye, and beyond that in my mind—was something alien. The lighted circle of pavement below me, the familiar front porches, and the dark mass of houses and town beyond them—were fearful. Now they were menacing, all these familiar things and faces; the town had changed or was changing into something very terrible, and was after me. It wanted me, too, and I knew it.

A stair tread creaked, there was the sound of a soft footstep, and I swung in the darkness, crouching low, my flashlight raised as a weapon. Quietly Jack said, "It's me," and I flicked on the light and saw his face, tired and still sleepy. When he'd stopped beside me, I turned the light off, and for some moments we stood looking out at Mill Valley. The sleeping house under our feet, the street outside, the entire town were still and deathly silent; low ebb time for the human body and spirit.

After a few minutes Jack murmured, "Been down-stairs lately?"

"Yeah," I said, then answered his unspoken questions. "Don't worry; they've each had a hundred cc's of air, intravenously."

"Dead?"

I shrugged. "If you can say that about something that's never been alive, really. In any case, they're reverting."

"Back to the gray stuff?"

I nodded, and in the starlight from the window, I saw Jack shiver. "Well," he said then, trying to keep his voice casual, "it was no delusion. The blanks are real. They duplicate living persons. Mannie was wrong."

"Yeah."

"Miles, what happens to the original when the blanks duplicate a man? Are there two of them walking around?"

"Obviously not," I said, "or we'd have seen them. I don't know what happens, Jack."

"And why should your patients all check in with you, trying to convince you nothing was wrong? They were lying, Miles."

I just shrugged; I was tired and irritable and I'd have snapped at Jack if I'd tried to answer.

"Well," he said then, sighing wearily as he spoke, "whatever is happening, we have to assume that it's still confined to Mill Valley and the immediate area, because if it isn't—" He shrugged, and didn't finish. Then he went on: "So every house and building, every enclosed space in the entire town, has got to be searched. Right away, Miles," he said quietly. "And every last man, woman, and child has got to be examined; just how and for what, I don't know. But that's got to be figured out, and then done—fast." He was silent, then he said, "The local or state police can't do it. They haven't the authority, and try to imagine explaining this to them, anyway. Miles, this is a *national* emergency." He turned to me. "It actually is, as real as any we've ever faced: It may be more than that; a threat new to history." Again he paused, and continued, his voice quiet, matter of fact, and very earnest. "So somebody, Miles—the Army, Navy, the FBI, I don't know who or what—but somebody has to move into this town as fast as we can get them here. And they'll have to declare martial law, a state of siege, or something—anything!

And then do whatever has to be done." His voice dropped. "Root this thing out, smash it, crush it, kill it."

We stood there a moment or so longer, while I thought of what might be lying all around us, under the roofs out there, hidden in secret places; and it wouldn't bear much thinking about. "There's some coffee downstairs," I said, and we turned toward the stairs.

In the kitchen I poured us each some coffee, then Jack sat down at the table, while I leaned back against the stove. "All right, Jack," I said then. "But how? What do we do? Telephone the President, or something? Just ring up the White House, and when he answers the phone tell him that out here in Mill Valley, which voted right in the last election, we've found some bodies, except they aren't really bodies but something else, we don't know what, and please send the Marines right away?"

Jack shrugged impatiently. "I don't know! But we've got to do *something*; we *have* to find a way to reach people who can act! Quit clowning; figure something."

I nodded. "All right; chain of command."

"What?"

Eyes narrowing, I stared at Jack, suddenly excited, because this was the answer. "Listen; who do you know in Washington? Someone who knows you, knows you're not crazy, and that when you tell this story you mean it, and it's true. Somebody who can start the ball rolling, and keep this moving up a notch at a time till it reaches someone who can do something!"

After a moment or so, Jack shook his head. "Nobody; I don't know a soul in Washington. Do you?"

"No"—I slumped back against the stove. "Write to your congressman." Then I remembered, and shrugged. "I do know one guy, at that; the only person in Washington I know in any kind of official capacity at all. Ben Eichler—he was an upperclassman when I started school. He's in the regular Army now, works in the Pentagon. But he's only a lieutenant-colonel; I don't know anyone else."

"He'll do," Jack said quickly. "The Army could handle this, and he's in it. Right in the Pentagon, and with a pretty good rank; at least he could speak to a general without being court-martialed."

"All right"—I nodded. "No harm trying him, at least; I'll phone him." I lifted my cup to my mouth, and took a sip of coffee.

Jack watched, scowling, the impatience rising up in him till it burst out. "Now! Damn it, Miles, *now!* What are you waiting for!" Then he said, "I'm sorry, but . . . Miles, we've got to *move!*"

"Okay." I set my cup down on the stove, then walked to the living room, Jack right behind me; then I picked up the phone and dialed *O*. "Operator," I said when she answered, and now I spoke very slowly and carefully, "I want to phone Washington, D.C., person-to-person, Lieutenant-Colonel Benjamin Eichler. I don't know his number, but it's in the book." I turned to Jack. "There's an extension in my bedroom," I said. "Go listen in."

In the phone at my ear, I heard the remote little beep-beep sounds, the tiny clicks, the faint electronic hummings and silences, then the ringing began in the little black disc at my ear.

The third ring was interrupted and Ben's voice sounded, clear and tiny, in my ear. "Hello?"

"Ben?" I realized that I'd raised my voice, the way people do in long-distance phone calls. "This is Miles Bennell, in California."

"Hi, Miles!" The voice was suddenly pleased and cheerful. "How are you?"

"Fine, Ben, swell. Did I wake you up?"

"Why, hell, no, Miles; it's five-thirty A.M. here. Why would I be sleeping?"

I smiled a little. "Well, I'm sorry, Ben, but it's time you were up. We taxpayers aren't paying your fancy salary to have you lie around in bed all day. Listen, Ben"—I spoke seriously—"have you got some time? A good half hour, maybe, to sit and listen to what I have to tell you? It's terribly important, Ben, and I want to explain it fully; I want to talk as though this were a local call. Can you give me some time, and listen carefully?"

"Sure; wait a second." There was a pause of several moments, then the clear, far-away voice said, "Go ahead, Miles, I'm all set."

I said, "Ben, you know me; you know me very well. I'll start by telling you I'm not drunk, you know I'm not insane, and you know I don't play foolish practical jokes on my friends in the middle of the night, or any other time. I've got something to tell you that's very hard to believe, but it's true, and I want you to realize that, while you listen. Okay?"

"Yeah, Miles." The voice was sober, waiting.

"About a week ago," I began slowly, "on a Thursday. . ." and then talking quietly and leisurely, I tried to tell him the entire story, beginning with Becky's first visit to my office, and winding up some twenty minutes later with the events of tonight right up to the present moment.

It isn't easy explaining a long, complicated story over the telephone, though, not seeing the other man's face. And we had bad luck with the connection. At first I heard Ben, and he heard me, as clearly as though we were next door to each other. But when I began telling him what had been happening here, the connection faded, Ben had to keep asking me to repeat, and I almost had to shout to make him understand me. You can't talk well, you can't even think properly, when you have to repeat every other phrase, and I signaled the operator and asked for a better connection. After a little delay, the connection was cleared up, but I'd hardly resumed when a sort of buzzing sound started in the receiver in my ear, and then I had to try to talk over that. Twice the connection was broken off completely, the dial tone suddenly humming in my ear, and finally I was mad and shouting at the operator. It wasn't a satisfactory conversation at all, and when I'd finished, I wondered how it all must have sounded to Ben, the width of a continent away.

He answered when I'd finished. "I see," he said slowly, then paused for a moment or so, thinking. "Well, Miles," he said then, "what do you want me to do?"

"I don't know, Ben"—the connection was pretty good at the moment—"but you can see that something has to be done; you can see that. Ben, get the story moving. Right away. Move it on up, in Washington, till it reaches someone who can do something."

He laughed, a forced laugh from the stomach. "Miles, remember me? I'm a lieutenant-colonel in the Pentagon building; I salute the janitor. Why me, Miles? Don't you know anyone here who could really—"

"*No*, damn it! I'd be talking to them if I did! Ben, it has to be somebody who *knows* me, and knows I'm not crazy. And I don't know anyone else; it has to be you. Ben, you've *got* to—"

"All right, all right—" his voice was placating. "I'll do what I can, do all I can. If it's what you really want, I'll give this whole story to my colonel within an hour; I'll go see him and wake him up; he lives here in Georgetown. I'll tell him just what you've told me, as well as I've followed it. And I'll add my own report that I know you well, that you're a sane, sober, intelligent citizen, and that I am personally certain you're speaking the truth, or believe that you are. But that's all I can do, Miles, absolutely all, even if it means the end of the world before noon."

Ben paused for a moment, and I could hear the electrical silence of the wires between us. Then he added quietly, "And, Miles, it won't do one bit of good. Because what do you expect him to do with that story? He's not imaginative, to put it mildly. And even if he were, the colonel's no man to stick his neck out; you know what I mean? He wants his star before he retires; maybe a couple of them. And he's very conscious, asleep or awake, of what goes into his service record. He's worked up a reputation ever since West Point for good, hard, practical common sense. Not brilliant, but sound, that's his specialty; you know the type." Ben sighed. "Miles, I can just see him going to his general with a story like this. He wouldn't trust me to sharpen a pencil from then on!"

Now it was my turn to say, "I see."

"Miles, I'll do it! If you want me to. But even if the impossible happened, even if the colonel took this to the brigadier, who took it to the major-general, who carried it on up to three- or four-star level, what the hell are *they* going to do with this? By that time it'll be a weird fourth- or fifth-hand story started by some fool of a lieutenant-colonel they've never heard of or seen. And *he* got the story in a phone call from some crackpot friend, a civilian, out in California somewhere. Do you see? Can you actually imagine this reaching a level where something could be done; and then having it actually done? My God, you know the Army!"

My voice was tired and defeated as I said, "Yeah." I sighed, and said, "Yeah, I see, Ben. And you're right."

"I'll do it, and to hell with my service record—that's not important—if you can see even a chance that it'll help at all. Because I believe you. I don't say it's impossible that you're being hoaxed in some way for some weird reason, but at least *something's* happening out there that ought to be looked into. And if you think I should—"

"No," I said, and now my voice was firm and definite. "No, Ben, forget it. I'd have known better myself, if I'd thought about it; because you're completely right; it would be useless. There just isn't any point in wrecking your service record when it wouldn't do one bit of good."

We talked for a minute or so longer, and Ben tried to think of something helpful and suggested getting in touch with the papers. But I pointed out that they'd treat the story like one more UFO item; probably be very cute and humorous about it. He suggested the FBI then. I said I'd think about it, promised to keep in touch with him, and all that, then we said good-bye and hung up. A moment or so later, Jack came down the stairs.

"Well?" he said, and I just shrugged; there wasn't anything to say. After a moment Jack said, "Want to try the FBI?"

I didn't know or much care at that point, and I just nodded at the telephone. "There's the phone; go ahead if you want to." And Jack opened the San Francisco phone book.

A few moments later, he dialed the number, and I

watched him—552-2155. Jack held the phone at an angle to his ear so I could hear, and I heard the ringing sound begin. It was interrupted, a man's voice said, "Hel—" and the line went dead; a moment later the dial tone began.

Jack dialed again, very carefully. He finished, and before the ringing could begin, the operator cut in. "What number are you calling, please?" Jack told her, and she said, "Just a moment, please." Then the ringing began; and it continued—ring, then a pause, ring, then a pause, for half a dozen times. "Your party does not answer," the operator said presently, in that mechanical telephone-company voice they use. For just a moment, Jack held the phone before him, staring at it; then he raised it to his mouth. "Okay," he said softly. "Never mind."

He looked up at me, and spoke quietly, his voice rigidly calm. "They won't let the call get through, Miles. There's someone there, we heard him answer, but they won't ring the number again for us. Miles, they've got the telephone office now, and God knows what else."

I nodded. "Looks like it," I said, and then the panic ripped loose in our minds.

CHAPTER

ELEVEN

We thought we were thinking, but actually we moved on wild mindless impulse. We had the women on their feet, blinking in the light, questioning us bewilderedly, but at the looks on our faces when we didn't reply, the panic leaped from us to them like a contagion. Then all of us rushed through the house, gathering up clothes; Jack had a butcher knife thrust into his belt, I took every cent of money I had in the place, and we found Theodora down in the kitchen, half dressed, packing canned goods into a small carton; I don't know what she thought she was doing.

We actually bumped into one another in hallways, on the stairs, and rushing out of rooms; it must have looked like an old-time silent-film comedy, only there was no laughter in it. We were running—out of that house, and out of that town, as fast as we could move. We were suddenly overwhelmed, not knowing what else to do, how to fight back, or against what. Something impossibly terrible, yet utterly real, was menacing us in a way beyond our comprehension or abilities; and we fled.

Theodora still in bedroom slippers, we were slamming into Jack's car on the dark, silent street just out of the pool of swaying light from the overhead street lamp, our foolish armfuls of clothes tossed into the back seat. The starter ground, the motor caught, then Jack squealed rubber, pulling away from the curb, and we weren't thinking at all, just running, running, running, till we were on U.S. 101, and Mill Valley eleven miles behind us.

Then, moving along over the almost deserted road I began to feel a return of some sort of ordered thinking, or at least the illusion of it. Successful rapid flight, the piling up of distance, becomes in itself a calming thing, an antidote for fear, and I turned to Becky in the back seat beside me, smiling, my mouth opening to speak. Then I saw she was asleep, her face pale and drained in the light from a passing car, and the fright roared up in me again, worse than ever, bursting in my brain in a silent explosion of pure panic.

I was shaking Jack's shoulder, shouting at him to stop, then we were jouncing off the dark road onto the narrow dirt-and-gravel shoulder. Jack's parking brake rasped, then, leaning far across Theodora, he brought his fist down on the glove-compartment button, it flew open, he fumbled inside it, then scrambled out of the car, his face wild and questioning. I was leaning past him, yanking his keys from the dashboard, then we were running toward the back of the car. But Jack ran on, down the narrow dirt shoulder, and I had my mouth open to yell at him, when he dropped to one knee, and I knew what he was doing.

Jack once had the back of his car smashed in

while he was changing a tire, and now it's second nature with him, when he stops off the road, to set out flares. One sputtered in his hand, now, then rose into smoky pink-red flame, and as Jack raised it high to jam the spike into the ground, I shoved a key into the lock of his trunk, twisting it frantically.

Then Jack had the keys, yanking them from the lock. He found the right one, inserted it, turned, then heaved up the lid of the trunk. And there they lay, in the advancing, retreating waves of flickering red light: two enormous pods already burst open in one or two places, and I reached in with both hands, and tumbled them out onto the dirt. They were weightless as children's balloons, harsh and dry on my palms and fingers. At the feel of them on my skin, I lost my mind completely, and then I was trampling them, smashing and crushing them under my plunging feet and legs, not even knowing that I was uttering a sort of hoarse, meaningless cry—"Unhh! Unhh! Unhh!"—of fright and animal disgust. The wind had the flares twisting the flames till they sputtered and choked, and on the high cutaway embankment beside me, I saw a giant shadow—mine —squirming and dancing in a wild flickering, insane caper, the whole nightmare scene bathed in a mad light the color of froth from a wound, and I think I came close to losing my mind.

Jack was yanking hard on my arm, dragging me away, and we turned to the trunk again. Jack pulled out the spare can of gasoline he carried. He got the top off, and there at the side of the road, in the pink washes of smoky light, he drenched those two great weightless masses, and they dissolved into a mushy pulp of nothingness. Then I had a flare, wrenching it from the ground, and, running back, I hurled it into the soupy mass lying there in the dirt and gravel.

Pulling away fast, the car bumping onto the road again, I looked back, and the flames suddenly shot high, five or six feet; orange flames in a pink wash of light, the thick, greasy smoke twisting and rolling away in the heat waves. Watching, as Jack shifted fast into second, and then into high, I saw the flames drop quickly and subside into a score of inch-high, blue-and-red flickering tongues, the smoke blood-pink once again. Suddenly they went out, or were lost to view over a small rise of ground.

And now I didn't even try to talk or think; none of us did; we were drained of thought and emotion. I just sat, holding Becky's hand, steering the car with my eyes, around the curves, up and down the hills, piling up distance, Becky silent and bolt upright beside me.

An hour or so later, the green neon *Vacancy* sign looking cold and unfriendly, we stopped at a motel, the Rancho Something-or-other. Jack got out, and as I opened my door, Becky leaned toward me and whispered, "Don't get me a room alone, Miles; I'm too scared. I just couldn't stay by myself tonight; I couldn't; I'm so scared." I nodded, and got out. We awakened the proprietor, a perpetually tired and irritated middle-aged woman in slippers and a robe, who had long since given up wondering about the people who woke her at any and all hours of the night. With no more than half a dozen words, we got two double rooms, paid for them, were given keys, and we signed the registration cards. Without consciously thinking about it, I signed a false name, then I noticed Jack doing the same thing, and realized why. It was idiotic, of course, but it seemed terribly important just then to make ourselves anonymous, and crawl into a hole and out of sight, no one in the world knowing where we were.

In the tumbled mound of clothes in the back seat,

Jack found pajamas, but I didn't, and borrowed a pair of his; both of the women found nightgowns. I unlocked the door of our room, ushered Becky in first, then stepped in after her. I'd asked for twin beds, but there stood a double bed, and when I made a sound of annoyance, and turned back to the door, Becky stopped me, a hand on my arm. "Leave it this way, Miles, please. I'm just too scared; I haven't been this frightened since I was a little girl. Oh, Miles, don't leave me!"

We were asleep in less than five minutes. I lay, not touching Becky, except for an arm around her waist, and she had both hands clasped over mine, holding it tight, like a child. And we slept, simply slept, for the rest of the night. We were tired; I'd had no sleep at all since three o'clock of the night before. Anyway, there's a time and place for everything, and while this may have been the place, it wasn't the time. We slept.

If I dreamed, no traces remained in my memory; I simply left the world and life for exhausted oblivion, and it was the best thing that could have happened to me. I might have slept on till noon, I think, but around eight-thirty, quarter to nine, I turned over, bumped into someone, and heard her sigh. My eyes flashed open as Becky, still asleep, turned to snuggle close to me.

It was too much. Wonderfully warm, flushed with sleep, the soft column of her breath pressing my cheek, she lay full length beside me, and I could no more have stopped gathering her into my arms than stop breathing. For a long, long moment, the warm length of her pressed against me, that was enough; and then it wasn't, and what happened with us now was the best thing that had happened to me for a very long time.

When I'd showered and dressed, feeling good, grinning at Becky, I went outside, and Jack was there, wandering the little paved parking area. We spoke, stood looking around at the morning, and then when our eyes met again, I said, "Well? What now? Where to?"

Jack looked at me, his face tired and drawn; then one shoulder lifted in a little shrug. "Home," he said. I stared at him.

"Yeah, that's right," he said irritably. "Where did you think we were going?" I was frowning, suddenly angry, my mouth opening to argue with him; but I didn't. After a moment, I closed my mouth, and Jack smiled a little, nodding as though I'd said something he agreed with. "Sure," he said, "you know it as well as I do. Did you think you were going to change your name, grow a beard, and go off somewhere to start life anew?"

I smiled a little too. When Jack put it into words, anything but going back home to Mill Valley was unreal, without force or conviction. It was morning now, the air bright with sun, I'd had half a night's sleep, and my brain was washed clear of horror again. The fear was there still, active and real, but I was able to think without panic. We'd had our running away, and it had done us good; me, anyway. But we belonged at home, not in some vague, unknown, mythical new place. And now it was time to go back, to the place we belonged, which belonged to us, and fight against whatever was happening, as best we could, and however we could. Jack knew it, and now so did I.

A moment later, Theodora came out, and walked toward us. As she got nearer, her eyes on Jack's face, she began to frown; then, stopping before him, she simply looked at him questioningly. Jack nodded. "Yeah," he said uneasily. "Honey, Miles and I feel—" He stopped as Theodora slowly nodded her head.

"Never mind," she said tiredly. "If you're going back, you're going back; it doesn't matter why. And where you go, I go." She shrugged, and turning to me, managed a wan smile. "'Morning, Miles."

When Becky came out, her nightgown and my pajamas rolled into a bundle under her arm, her face was anxious and intent, full of what she had to say. "Miles" —she stopped in front of us—"I've got to go back. It's all real, it really is happening and my father—" She stopped talking as I nodded.

"We're all going back," I said gently, taking her elbow, leading her toward the car, Jack and Theodora walking along with us. "Only first, for God's sake, let's get us some breakfast."

At two minutes after eleven that morning, Jack shifted into second and began to curse, as we turned off the freeway onto the road into Mill Valley, and the last few miles to home. We were charged with a terrible urgency to get there, now—to move, to act—but the road had deteriorated, no repairs made for some time now, and it was scattered with sharp-edged little chuckholes, and occasional bigger ones that could break an axle if you hit them too fast. Mill Valley is isolated, only a few ways into it, and this was happening to all the roads; they go fast if you don't keep them up, and we cursed the city council, the county, and whoever else we thought might be responsible.

CHAPTER

TWELVE

I don't know how many people still live in the town they were born in, these days. But I did, and it's inexpressibly sad to see that place die; maybe even worse than the death of a friend, because you have other friends to turn to. We did a great deal, and a lot of things happened, in the hour and fifty-five minutes that followed; and in every minute of it my sense of loss deepened and my sense of shock grew at what we saw, and I knew that something dear to me was lost. Moving along an outlying street, now, I had my first actual feeling of the terrible change in Mill Valley, and I remembered something an uncle had once told me about the war, the fighting in Italy. They would come, sometimes, into a town supposedly free of Germans, the population supposedly friendly. But they'd enter with rifles at the ready just the same, glancing around, up, and back, with every cautious step. And they saw every window, door, alleyway, and face, he'd told me, as something to fear. Now, home again in the town I was born in—I'd delivered papers on this very street—I knew how he'd felt entering those Italian villages; I was afraid of what I might see and find here.

Jack said, "I'd like to run up to our place for a few minutes, Miles; Teddy and I need some clothes."

I didn't want to go with them; I was sick with the thoughts and feelings moving through me, and I knew I had to see this town, to look at it up close, hoping to be able to tell myself that it was still the way it always had been. I had no Saturday office hours to worry about, another doctor on call this weekend, so I said, "Let us out, then, Jack, and we'll walk. I feel like it, if Becky doesn't mind, and we'll meet you at my place."

So Jack let us out on Sycamore Avenue, maybe a ten-minute walk from my house. Sycamore is a quiet residential street, like most of the others in Mill Valley, and as the sound of Jack's car died, Becky and I walked along toward Throckmorton, and there wasn't a soul in sight, and hardly a sound but our shoes on the walk; it should have seemed peaceful.

Not talking much, we walked for half a dozen blocks, and I looked around me. I'd driven the streets of Mill Valley every day; I'd been in this very block not a week before. And everything I was seeing now had been here to see then, except that—you don't really see the familiar until it's thrust upon you, you don't actually notice, until there's a reason to do so. But now there was a reason, and I looked around me, really seeing the street and the houses along it, trying to soak up every impression they could give me.

I couldn't possibly describe any specific way in which anything I saw seemed different; yet things did, in a way words can't explain. But if I were an artist, painting the way Sycamore Street seemed to me, walking along now with Becky, I think I'd distort the windows of the houses we passed. I'd show them with half-drawn shades, the bottom edge of each shade curving downward, so that the windows looked like heavy-lidded, watchful eyes, quietly and terribly aware of us as we passed through that silent street. I'd show the porch rails and stair rails hugging the old houses like protective arms, sullenly guarding them against our curiosity. I'd paint the houses themselves as huddled and crouching, alien and withdrawn, resentful, evil, and full of icy malice against the two figures walking along the street between them. And somehow I'd depict the very trees and lawns, the street and sky above us, as dark— though it was actually clear and sunny—and give the picture a brooding, silent, fearful quality. And I think I'd make every color just a shade off-key.

I don't know if that would convey what I felt, but —something was wrong, and I knew it. And then I knew that Becky did, too.

"Miles," she said in a cautious, lowered tone, "am I imagining it, or does this street look—dead?"

I shook my head. "You're not wrong. In seven blocks we haven't passed a single house with as much as the trim being repainted; not a roof, porch, or even a cracked window being repaired; not a tree, shrub, or a blade of grass being planted, or even trimmed. Nothing's happening, Becky, nobody's doing anything. And they haven't for days, maybe weeks."

It was true; we walked three more blocks, to Blithedale, and then onto Throckmorton, and saw not a sign of change. We might have been on a finished stage set, completed to the last nail and final stroke of a brush. Yet you can't walk for blocks on an ordinary street inhabited by human beings without seeing evidences of, say, a garage being built, a new cement sidewalk being laid, a yard being spaded, a new window being installed—at least some little signs of the endless urge to change and improve that marks the human race.

We turned onto Throckmorton, and while there were people on the sidewalks, and cars beside the parking meters, somehow the street seemed surprisingly empty and inactive. Except for the occasional slam of a car door, or the sound of a voice, the street was very nearly silent for as much as half a block at a time; the way it is late at night, with the town asleep.

A great deal of what we saw then, I'd seen before, driving along Throckmorton, on my way to house calls; but I hadn't really noticed, hadn't really looked at this street I'd been seeing all my life. But I did now, and I suddenly remembered the empty store I'd seen near my office. Because now, in the first few blocks—our footsteps plainly audible on the walk—we passed three more empty stores. The windows had been whitened, and through them, dimly, we could see the interiors littered and uncleaned, and they looked as though they'd been empty for some time now. We passed under the *Mill Town Tavern* sign, and the letters *rn* in *Tavern* were missing. The windows were flyspecked, the cardboard liquor signs badly sunfaded. There was only one customer, sitting motionless at the bar—the doors were open, and we glanced in as we passed—and the place was silent.

The Inn Place was closed up—for good, apparently, because the counter stools were unbolted and lying on their sides on the floor. A shoe store still had some Fourth-of-July advertising in the window, some children's shoes grouped around it, and over the shine of their leather lay a fine layer of dust. The Sequoia theater, when we came to it, had a placard in an outside display case, and it read *Open Saturday and Sunday Evenings Only.*

I noticed again, as Becky and I walked along the street, how much paper and litter there was; the city trash baskets stood full, and torn sheets of newspaper and tiny drifts of dust lay in the corners of store entrances, and at the bases of street lamps and mailboxes. In the little town square the weeds were high, untended for days. Becky murmured, "The popcorn wagon's gone," and I saw that it was; for years a red wheeled, glass-and-gilt popcorn wagon had stood beside the bus station daytimes, and now it and Eddie, the middle-aged man who owned and ran it, were gone.

Dave's Diner lay just ahead; the last time I'd eaten there I'd wondered vaguely why there'd been so few customers. And now I wondered again, as we stopped to glance in through the plate glass, for only two people were having lunch at a time when it should have been crowded. Fastened to the window, as always, was the day's menu, photocopied daily, and I looked at it. There was a choice of three entrées, and for years they'd always had six or eight.

"Miles, when did all this *happen?*" Becky gestured to indicate the length of the semideserted street behind and ahead of us.

"A little at a time," I said, and shrugged. "We're just realizing it now; the town's dying."

We turned away from the restaurant window, and Ed Burley's plumbing truck passed, and he waved, and we waved back. Then, in that queer silence that occasionally came over the street, we could hear our footsteps on the sidewalk again.

At the corner, at Lovelock's Pharmacy, Becky said, trying to sound casual, "Let's have a Coke, or some coffee, or something," and I nodded, and we turned in. I knew she wanted, not a Coke or coffee, but to get off this street for a minute or so; and so did I.

There was a man sitting at the counter, which surprised me. Then I was surprised that I should have been surprised; but somehow, after our walk down Throckmorton, I'd almost have expected any place we might have gone in to to be empty. The man turned to glance at us, and I recognized him. He was a salesman from some San Francisco wholesale house; I'd once treated him for a twisted ankle. We took the two stools next to him and I said, "How's business?" Old Mr. Lovelock looked at me inquiringly from down the counter, and I held up two fingers and said, "Two Cokes."

"Lousy," the man next to me answered. There was still the remainder of a smile on his face from our greeting, but it seemed to me that a hint of hostility had come into his face. "At least in Mill Valley," he added. Then he sat looking at me for several moments, as though debating whether to say any more; down the counter, the spigot coughed as our Coke glasses were filled. Then the man beside me leaned toward me, lowered his voice, and said, "What the hell's going on around here?"

Mr. Lovelock came carrying our Cokes, then he set them down carefully and slowly, and stood there for a moment or so, blinking benignly. I waited till he turned away and shuffled off to the back of the store again before I answered. "How do you mean?" I said casually, and took a sip of my Coke. It tasted bad; it was too warm and it hadn't been stirred, and though I looked around, there wasn't a spoon or straw in sight; and I set the glass down on the counter.

"You can't get an order any more." The salesman shrugged. "Not to amount to anything, anyway. Just the staples, the bare essentials, but none of the extras." He remembered, then, that you mustn't knock the home-town to a resident; and he smiled jovially. "You people on a buyers' strike, or something?" He gave up the effort, and quit smiling. "People just aren't buying," he muttered sullenly.

"Well, I guess things are a little tight around here at the moment, that's all."

"Maybe." He picked up his cup and swished the coffee around in the bottom of it, staring morosely down at the cup. "All I know is it's hardly worth coming into town lately. Hell of a place to get to now, for one thing; takes time just to get in and out of Mill Valley. And for all the good I do, I might as well pick up what orders they got by phone. And it isn't just me," he added defensively. "Everyone else says so, the other sales-men. Most of them have quit coming around; you can't make gas money in this town any more. You can hardly even buy a Coke most places, or"—he nodded at his coffee cup—"a cup of coffee. Twice, lately, this place has been out of coffee altogether, for no reason at all, and today when they have it, it's lousy, terrible." He finished the coffee in a gulp, making a face, and as he slid off the counter stool the hostility was plain in his face, and he didn't bother to smile. "What's the mat-ter," he said angrily, "this town dying on its feet?" He pulled a coin from his pocket, leaned forward to lay it on the counter, and, his face close to mine, spoke quietly into my ear, with suppressed bitterness. "They act as though they don't even want salesmen around." For a moment he stared at me, then he smiled profes-sionally. "See you, Doc," he said, nodded politely at Becky, then turned and walked to the door.

"Miles," Becky said, and I turned to look at her. "Listen, Miles"—she spoke in a whisper, but her voice was tense—"do you think it's possible for a town to cut itself off from the world? Gradually discourage people from coming around, till it's not noticed any more? Actually almost forgotten?"

I thought about it, then shook my head. "No."

"But the roads, Miles! They're getting almost impassable; that doesn't make sense! And that salesman, and the way the town looks—"

"It's impossible, Becky; it'd take a whole town to do that, every soul in it. It'd have to be absolutely unanimous in decision, and action. And that would include us."

"Well," she said, "they tried to include us."

For a moment I stared at her; she was right. "Come on," I said then, laid a dollar on the counter, and stood up. "Let's get out of here; we've seen what we came to see."

At the next corner, we passed my office, and I looked up at my name in gold leaf on the second-story window; it seemed a long time since I'd been there. We walked on, out of the shopping area, and Becky said, "I've got to stop in at my house and see my father, and, Miles, I hate to; I can hardly bear seeing him the way he is now."

There was nothing I could say to that, and I simply nodded. A block or so ahead of us now, lay the public library, and I said, "We'll have to take a minute to stop in at the library."

Miss Weygand was at the desk as we walked in, and I smiled with real pleasure, as always. She'd been librarian since I was a grade-school kid coming in for *Tom Swift* and Zane Grey books, and she was the opposite of the conventional notion of what a librarian usually is. She was a gray-haired, intelligent-eyed, brisk little woman, and you could talk in the main reading room of her library, if you weren't too loud about it, and there were comfortable cushioned chairs beside low magazine-strewn tables. It was a nice place to spend a pleasant hour or afternoon, a place where people met friends to talk quietly. She was wonderful with children—had an enormous natural and interested patience—and as a kid, I always remembered, you felt welcome there, and not an intruder.

Miss Weygand was one of my favorite people, and now as we stopped at her desk, and greeted her, she smiled, a bright really pleased smile that made you glad you were here. "Hello, Miles," she said. "Glad to see you're reading again," and I grinned. "It's nice to see you, Becky," she said. "Say hello to your dad for me."

We replied, then I said, "Could we look at *The Mill Valley Record* files, Miss Weygand? For last summer; the first part of July."

"Certainly," she said, and when I offered to go downstairs for the file myself, she said, "No, sit down and relax; I'll bring it up."

We took a couple chairs at the magazine table, Becky picked up a magazine, and I sat glancing around; only one other person, an elderly man at another table, was here, which was unusual. It took awhile before Miss Weygand came up from the file room; it was twelve-twenty before she reappeared, smiling, with the big, cloth-covered newspaper-sized book stamped *Mill Valley Record, July, August, September, 1976*. She laid it on the table between us, and we thanked her; the date line on Jack's clipping had been July 9, and I opened the big book, and found the *Record* for the day before.

Both of us scanned the front page, glancing carefully at each story; there was nothing there about giant seed pods or Professor L. Bernard Budlong, and I turned the page. In the upper left corner of page three was a rectangular hole, two columns wide by five or six inches deep; a news story had been neatly sliced out with a razor blade, and Becky and I glanced at each other, then examined the rest of the page, and page two. We found nothing of what we were looking for, nor did we find it in the remaining three pages of the July 8 *Record*.

We turned to the July 7 issue and began with page one. There was nothing in the paper about Budlong or the pods. On the bottom half of the July 6 *Record*'s first page was a hole seven or eight inches long and three columns wide. On the bottom half of the July 5 issue was another hole just about as long but only two columns wide.

It wasn't a guess, but a sudden stab of direct intuitive knowledge—I *knew*, that's all—and I swung in my chair to stare across the room at Miss Weygand. She stood motionless behind the big desk, her eyes fastened on us, and in the instant I swung to look at her, her face was wooden, devoid of any expression, and the eyes were bright, achingly intent, and as inhumanly cold as the eyes of a shark. The moment was less than a moment—the flick of an eyelash—because instantly she smiled, pleasantly, inquiringly, her brows lifting in polite question. "Anything I can do?" she said with the calm, interested eagerness typical of her in all the years I had known her.

"Yes," I said. "Would you come here, please, Miss Weygand?"

Smiling brightly, she walked around her desk and crossed the room toward us. There was no one else in the library now; it was twenty-six minutes past twelve by the big clock over her desk, and the only other patron had left a few minutes before.

Miss Weygand stopped beside me, I glanced up at her, and she stood looking down at me, her expression pleasantly inquiring. I nodded at the hole on the front page of the newspaper before me. "Just before you brought us this file," I said quietly, "you cut out all references to the seed pods found here last summer, didn't you?"

She frowned—bewildered by this accusation—and leaned forward to stare down in surprise at the mutilated paper on the low round table.

Then I stood up to face her, my face a few inches from hers. I said, "Don't bother, Miss Weygand, or whatever you are. Don't bother to put on an act for me." I leaned closer, staring her directly in the eyes, and my voice dropped. "I know you," I said softly. "I know what you are."

For a moment she still stood, glancing helplessly from me to Becky in utter bewilderment; then suddenly she dropped the pretense. Gray-haired Miss Weygand, who twenty years ago had loaned me the first copy of *Huckleberry Finn* I ever read, looked at me, her face going wooden and blank, with an utterly cold and pitiless alienness. There was nothing there now, in that gaze, nothing in common with me; a fish in the sea had more kinship with me than this staring thing before me. Then she spoke. *I know you*, I'd said, and now she replied, and her voice was infinitely remote and uncaring. "Do you?" she said, then turned on her heel and walked away.

I gestured at Becky and we walked on out of the library. Outside, on the sidewalk, we took half a dozen steps in silence, then Becky shook her head. "Even her," she murmured, "even Miss Weygand," and the tears shone in her eyes. "Oh, Miles," she said softly, and glanced around, first over one shoulder, then the other, at the houses, quiet lawns, and the street beside us, "how many more?" I didn't know the answer to that, and I just shook my head, and we walked on, toward Becky's house.

CHAPTER

THIRTEEN

There was a car parked in front of Becky's and as we approached, we recognized it: a 1973 Buick Century sedan, the blue paint faded from the sun. "Wilma, Aunt Aleda, and Uncle Ira," Becky murmured, and looked at me. Then she said, "Miles"—we were almost at the house, and she stopped on the sidewalk—"I can't go in there!"

I stood for a moment, thinking. "We won't go in," I said then, "but we've got to see them, Becky." She started shaking her head, and I said, "We've got to know what's going *on*, Becky! We have to find out! Or we might as well not have come back to town." I took her arm, and we turned in at the brick walk leading up to the house, but I stepped off it immediately, pulling Becky off, too, and we walked in silence on the lawn beside it. "Where would they be?" I said. When she didn't answer, I shook her once, almost roughly, my hand still on her arm. "Becky, where would they be? The living room?"

She nodded dumbly, and we walked silently around to the side of the house, and the wide old porch that passed under the living-room windows. The windows were open, we heard the murmur of voices, behind the white living-room curtains, and I stopped, lifted a foot, pulled off my shoe, then took off the other. I glanced down at Becky, and she swallowed; then, holding to my arm, she pulled off her shoes, and just beyond the living-room windows, toward the back of the house, we crept silently up the porch stairs. Then, beside the open window, we sat down on the porch, very carefully and slowly. We were out of sight, completely sheltered from the street by the big old trees and high shrubbery of the lawn.

"... like some more coffee?" we heard a voice, Becky's father, saying.

"No," said Wilma, and we heard the clink of a cup and saucer set down on a wood surface, "I've got to be back at the shop by one. But you and Uncle Ira can stay, Aunt Aleda."

"No," Wilma's aunt replied, "we'll get along, too. Sorry to have missed seeing Becky."

I moved my head to bring an eye just above the window sill, at the side of the open window. There they sat: Becky's gray-haired father, smoking a cigar; round-faced, red-cheeked Wilma; tall old Uncle Ira; and the tiny, sweet-faced old lady who was Wilma's aunt; all of them looking and sounding precisely the way they always had. I turned to glance at Becky, wondering if we hadn't made some terrible mistake, and if these people weren't just what they seemed.

"I'm sorry, too," Becky's father replied. "I thought surely she'd be home; she's back in town, you know."

"Yes, we know," said Uncle Ira, "and so is

Miles," and I wondered how they could possibly know we were back, or that we'd even been gone. Then something happened, without warning, that made the hair on the back of my neck prickle and stand erect.

This is very hard to explain, but—when I was in college, a middle-aged black man had a shoeshine stand, on the sidewalk before one of the older hotels, and he was a town character. Everyone patronized Billy, because he was everyone's notion of what a "character" should be. He had a title for each regular customer. "'Mornin', Professor," he'd say soberly to a thin glasses-wearing businessman who sat down for a shoeshine each day. "A greetin' to you, Captain," he'd say to someone else. "Howdydo, Colonel," "Nice evenin', Doctor," "General, I'm pleased to see you." The flattery was obvious, and people always smiled to show they weren't taken in by it; but they liked it just the same.

Billy professed a genuine love for shoes. He'd nod with approving criticalness when you showed up with a new pair. "Good leather," he'd murmur, nodding with a considered conviction, "pleasure to work on shoes like these," and you'd feel a glow of foolish pride in your own good taste. If your shoes were old, he might hold one cupped in his hand when he'd finished with it, twisting it a little from side to side to catch the light. "Nothin' takes a shine like good aged leather, Lieutenant, *nothin'*." And if you ever showed up with a cheap pair of shoes, his silence gave conviction to his compliments of the past. With Billy, the shoeshine man, you had the feeling of being with that rarest of persons, a happy man. He obviously took contentment in one of the simpler occupations of the world, and the money involved seemed actually unimportant. When you put them into his hands, he didn't even look at the coins you had given him; his acceptance was absent-minded, his attention devoted to your shoes, and to you, and you walked away feeling a little glow, as though you'd just done a good deed.

One night I was up till dawn, in a student escapade of no importance now, and, alone in my old car, I found myself in the run-down section of town, a good two miles from the campus. I was suddenly aching for sleep, too tired to drive on home. I pulled to the curb, and, with the sun just beginning to show, I curled up in the back seat under the old blanket I kept there. Maybe half a minute later, nearly asleep, I was pulled awake again by steps on the sidewalk beside me, and a man's voice said quietly, "'Morning, Bill."

My head below the level of the car window, I couldn't see who was talking, but I heard another voice, tired and irritable, reply, "Hi, Charley," and the second voice was familiar, though I couldn't quite place it. Then it continued, in a suddenly strange and altered tone. "'Mornin', Professor," it said with a queer, twisted heartiness. "'Mornin'!" it repeated. "Man, just *look* at those shoes. You had them shoes—lemme see, now!—fifty-six years come Tuesday, and they still takes a lovely shine!" The voice was Billy's, the words and tone those the town knew with affection, but—parodied, and a shade off key. "Take it easy, Bill," the first voice murmured uneasily, but Billy ignored it. "I just love those shoes, Colonel," he continued in a suddenly vicious, jeering imitation of his familiar patter. "That's all I want, Colonel, just to handle people's shoes. Le'me kiss 'em! Please le'me kiss your feet!" The pent-up bitterness of years tainted every word and syllable he spoke. And then, for a full minute perhaps, standing there on a sidewalk of the slum he lived in, Billy went

CHAPTER

FOURTEEN

A great deal of Marin County, California, is hilly, and Mill Valley is built on and among a series of hills, the streets winding through or curving over them. I knew all of them, every foot of every street and hill, and now I headed for a little dead-end street maybe three blocks from Budlong's address. It ended at a hill too steep for building, and overgrown with weeds, underbrush, and scrubby eucalyptus. We reached it, and parked beside a clump of small trees, more or less out of sight. Only two houses had a direct view of the car, and it was always possible that no one in them had seen us. We got out, and I left my ignition key in the car, the motor running. We were through with the car, and anyone finding it with the motor on might just possibly waste time waiting for us to come back. There was simply no way I could carry Nick's pistol without it showing, and after a moment I threw it into the weeds.

We climbed the hill then, along a path I'd followed

been meaning to stop in and see you about—what happened." Then she laughed falsely, in a hideous burlesque of embarrassment.

Tiny little Aunt Aleda tittered, and picked up Wilma's conversation with me. "I've been *so* embarrassed, Miles. I don't quite know what happened"—the nastiness in her tone was actually sickening—"or how to tell you, but . . . I've come to my senses again." Now the little old lady's voice deepened. "Don't bother to explain, Wilma"—she was imitating my tone and manner to perfection. "I don't want you to worry, or feel badly; just forget the whole thing."

Then they all laughed—soundlessly—their lips pulled back from their teeth, their eyes amused, mocking, and utterly cold; and I knew these weren't Wilma, Uncle Ira, Aunt Aleda, or Becky's father, knew they were not human beings at all, and I was very nearly sick. Becky sat flat on the floor of the porch, her back supported by the wall of the house, and her face was completely drained of blood, and her mouth hung open, and I knew she was only semiconscious.

I pinched up a fold of skin on her forearm between my thumb and forefinger, then twisted it hard, at the same time clapping my other hand tight over her mouth, so that she couldn't cry out from the sudden pain. Watching her face closely, I saw a little rush of color come into her cheeks, and with my knuckles I rapped her sharply on the forehead where the skin is thin, hurting her so the anger flashed in her eyes. Then I crossed my lips with a forefinger, put a hand on her elbow, and helped her to stand. We made no sound as we moved down off the porch in stocking-feet, carrying our shoes. At the sidewalk, we put them on—I didn't stop to tie my laces—and walked ahead toward my house two blocks beyond. All Becky said was, "Oh,

Miles," in a sick, subdued sort of moan, and I just nodded, and we kept on, walking fast, putting distance between us and that corrupted old house.

We were halfway up my front steps before I noticed the figure on my porch swing; then his movement, as he started to rise, caught my eye, and I saw the brass buttons and blue uniform coat. "Hi, Miles, Becky," he said quietly; it was Nick Grivett, the local police chief, and he was smiling pleasantly.

"Hello, Nick." I made my voice casual and inquiring. "Anything wrong?"

"No"—he shook his head. "Not a thing." He stood there, across the porch, a middle-aged man smiling benignly. "Would like you to come down to the station, though—my office, that is—if you don't mind, Miles."

"Sure"—I nodded. "What's up, Nick?"

He moved a shoulder slightly. "Nothing much. Few questions is all."

But I wouldn't let it go. "About what?"

"Oh"—again he shrugged. "For one thing, that body you and Belicec say you found—just want to get the record straight on that."

"Okay." I turned to Becky. "Want to come?" I said, as though it weren't important. "Won't take long, will it, Nick?"

"No." His voice was casual. "Ten, fifteen minutes maybe."

"All right. Take my car?"

"Rather use mine, Miles, if you don't mind. I'll run you back when we're through." He nodded toward the side of the house. "I parked in your garage, next to your car, Miles; you left the doors open."

I nodded as though that were natural, but of course it wasn't. The natural, easy place to park was in the street, unless you were afraid the gold star on your car might scare away the people you were waiting for. I stepped politely back to the porch rail, motioning Nick to precede me, and yawned a little, bored and uninterested. Nick walked forward toward the stairs, a squat, heavily built, plump little man, his jaw no higher than my shoulder. In the instant he stepped before me, I brought up my fist as hard as I could, and hit him a terrible blow on the jaw. But it isn't as easy to knock out a man with a blow as you might think, unless you're trained and expert at it, and I wasn't.

Nick staggered sideways, and went down, to his knees. Then I had an arm around his neck, standing at his back, pulling his chin up in the crook of my elbow over my hip, and he had to stumble to his feet to ease the pressure on his throat. I saw his face, his head bent far back as I curved my hip into his back, and while you'd expect a man to be angry, his eyes were cold, hard, and as empty of emotion as a barracuda's. I pulled out his gun, rammed it into his back, and let him go, and he knew I'd use it, and stood still. Then I handcuffed his hands behind his back with his own cuffs, and took him into the house.

Becky touched my arm. "Miles, this is too much for us. They're after us, all of them, and they'll get us. Miles, we've got to leave; we've got to *run*."

I took her by both arms, just above the elbows, staring down into her face, and I nodded. "Yeah—I want you out of here, Becky. Out of this town, and a thousand miles away, and I want you to take my car right now. I'll run, too. But I'll be running and fighting at the same time—right here. Don't worry about me; I'll be keeping out of their way; but I've got to stay here. I want you out of the way, though, and safe."

She stared back at me, bit her lip, then shook her head. "I don't want safety without you. What good is that?" I started to speak, but she said, "Don't argue, Miles; there just isn't *time.*"

After a moment I said, "All right," pushed Grivett into a chair, then picked up the phone, and dialed Mannie Kaufman's number; it seemed to me now that we needed all the help we could get.

The phone rang at the other end of the line, the third ring was interrupted, I heard Mannie's voice say, "Hel—"; then the line went dead. A moment later the operator, in the telephone-company voice they use, said, "What number are you calling, please?" I told her, the ringing began again, and kept on, and this time there was no answer. I knew she'd simply plugged me into a ringing circuit, and that Mannie's phone wasn't ringing, and neither was anyone else's.

I broke the connection, dialed Jack's number, and when he answered, I knew they'd allowed this call to go through to listen in on whatever we said, and I spoke fast. "Jack, there's trouble; they tried to get us, and they'll try to get you. Better get out of there fast; we're leaving my house the minute I hang up."

"All right, Miles. Where you going?"

I had to stop and think how to say this to Jack. I wanted anyone else listening to think I was leaving town, that we all were. And I needed a way to say that to Jack so he'd know it wasn't true. He's a literary man, and I tried to think of some figure in literature whose name was a symbol for falsehood, but for the moment I couldn't. Then I remembered—a Biblical name: Ananias, the liar. "Well, Jack," I said, "there's a woman I know runs a small hotel a couple hour's drive from here: Mrs. Ananias. You recognize the name?"

"Yeah, Miles," Jack said, and could tell he was smiling. "I know Mrs. Ananias, and her reputation for reliability."

"Well, believe me, Jack, you can rely on this just as much: Becky and I are leaving town, right now, and to hell with it. We're going to Mrs. Ananias's place; you understand me, Jack? You know what we're going to do?"

"Perfectly," he said. "I understand you perfectly" —and I knew that he did, and that he knew we were leaving my house, but were not leaving town. "I think we'll do exactly the same thing," he said, "so why don't we all go together? Suggest a place to meet, Miles."

"Well," I said, "remember the man in your newspaper clipping? The teacher?" I knew Jack would know I meant Budlong, and while I was talking, I was leafing through the phone book, hunting up his address. "He's got something we have to have; it's the only next step I can think of. We'll stop by there, and I think maybe we'll arrive on foot. Meet us there with your car; drive past in exactly one hour."

"Fine," he said, and hung up, and I could only hope we'd fooled whoever was listening.

Out in the garage, I found Grivett's tiny handcuff key on his key chain. My gun in his side while he knelt on the floor of his car in back, I unlocked his cuffs just long enough to loop them around a metal floor post of the front seat. Then I snapped them on again, chaining him to the floor of his car, in the back where he couldn't reach the horn. I wrapped his pistol in his cap, and with the butt of the gun—not the end of the butt, but the side—hit him hard on the head. You read a lot about people being hit on the head and knocked out, but you don't read much about blood clots in the brain. In actual fact, though, it's a delicate matter, hitting a man on the head, and while this may not have been Nick Grivett, not any more, it still looked like him, and I could not smash in his skull. He slumped as I hit him, and lay motionless. With my thumb and forefinger, I grabbed a fold of loose skin at the back of his neck and wrenched it hard; he yelped, and I brought the gun down again, carefully but just a bit harder. Again he lay motionless, and I twisted his skin harder than ever, watching his face for even a flicker of pain, but this time he didn't stir.

We backed out of the garage in my car, I got out and closed the garage doors, then we backed into the street and swung north toward East Blithedale Avenue and the home of L. Bernard Budlong, the man who might have the answer we didn't. Time was running out, was working against us, and I knew it. At any moment a police car, or any other car on the street, might suddenly force us to the curb, and I had Nick Grivett's gun lying ready on the seat beside me. I wanted to run, I wanted to hide, and the last thing I wanted to do was to sit talking in the home of some college professor, but we had to; I didn't know what else to do next. But I was terribly conscious of the red Mercedes we were riding in—Doc Bennell's car, as everyone in town knew—and I wondered if phones were being lifted in the houses we passed, and if the air at this moment wasn't filled with messages about us.

CHAPTER

FOURTEEN

A great deal of Marin County, California, is hilly, and Mill Valley is built on and among a series of hills, the streets winding through or curving over them. I knew all of them, every foot of every street and hill, and now I headed for a little dead-end street maybe three blocks from Budlong's address. It ended at a hill too steep for building, and overgrown with weeds, underbrush, and scrubby eucalyptus. We reached it, and parked beside a clump of small trees, more or less out of sight. Only two houses had a direct view of the car, and it was always possible that no one in them had seen us. We got out, and I left my ignition key in the car, the motor running. We were through with the car, and anyone finding it with the motor on might just possibly waste time waiting for us to come back. There was simply no way I could carry Nick's pistol without it showing, and after a moment I threw it into the weeds.

We climbed the hill then, along a path I'd followed

more than once as a kid, hunting small game with a .22 rifle. On the path no one more than a dozen feet away could see us, and I knew how to follow this path and others, keeping just below the crests of this hill and the next, to reach Budlong's back yard.

Presently his house lay below us, at the base of the hill we stood on. I'd found a spot, a dozen yards off the path, where we got a clear view, through the trees and brush, of his house and the yard in back of it. Now we studied it: a two-story house of brown-stained, wood-shingled siding, and a good-sized yard enclosed at the rear and one side by a high grape-stake fence, and by a tall row of shrubbery on the other side. "Outdoor living" is a big thing in California, and everyone who can has space for it on his property, private and sheltered from all eyes, and right now I was grateful for that. Nothing moved, no one was in sight, in the house and yard below, and so we came quietly down the hill, opened the high gate in the back fence, then crossed the yard, and walked around the side of the house, unseen, I felt certain, by anyone.

The house had a side entrance; I knocked, and as we stood waiting it occurred to me for the first time that Budlong might very well not be home, that quite likely he wasn't. He was, though; eight or ten seconds later, a man—in his middle or late thirties, I thought—appeared at the door, looked at us through the glass, then unbolted and opened it. He looked at me questioningly, wondering, I imagined, why we'd used the side door. "We got confused," I said, with a polite little laugh. "Guess we used the wrong door. Professor Budlong?"

"Yes," he said, and smiled pleasantly. He wore steel-rimmed glasses, had brownish, slightly wavy hair, and the kind of intelligent, interested, young-looking face that teachers so often seem to have.

"I'm Miles Bennell, Doctor Bennell, and—"

"Oh, yes." He nodded, smiling. "I've seen you around town, and—"

"I've seen you, too," I said. "I knew you were with the College, but didn't know your name. This is Becky Driscoll."

"How do you do." He opened the door wider, and stood to one side. "Come in, won't you?"

He led us in, then took us along a hall to a sort of study. He had an old-fashioned roll-top desk in there, some books in a hanging wall shelf, framed diplomas and photographs on the wall, a rug on the floor, and a battered old couch along one wall. It was a small room, with only one window, and rather dark. But the desk lamp was on, and the room had a sheltered, pleasant feeling; I imagined he spent a lot of time in it, working. Becky and I sat down on the couch, Budlong took the swivel desk chair, and swung part way around to face us. Again he smiled, a kind of friendly boyish smile. "What can I do for you?"

I told him. For reasons too long and complicated to explain, I said, we were very interested in anything he could tell us about a newspaper story in which he'd been quoted, though we hadn't seen the story, but only a reference to it in the *Record*.

He was grinning by the time I was finished, shaking his head in a sort of rueful amusement at himself. "That thing," he said. "I guess I'll never hear the end of it. Well"—he leaned back, slouching down to rest his neck on the back of his chair—"it was my own fault, so I shouldn't complain. What do you want to know, what the story said?"

"Yes," I answered. "And anything else you can add."

"Well"—he shrugged a shoulder—"the story said

some things it shouldn't have." He smiled again, at himself. "Newspaper reporters," he said ruefully. "I guess I've lived a sheltered life; I never met one before. This one, this young man, Beekey—he's an intelligent boy—phoned me one morning. I was professor of botany and biology, was I not? I said yes, and he asked if I'd drive out to what's still called the Parnell Barn, the little that's left of it. There was something I ought to see, he said, and he described what it was in just enough detail to arouse my curiosity."

Professor Budlong brought his hands together over his chest, the finger tips of one hand touching the tips of the other, and it occurred to me that professors must get so they unconsciously act the way people think professors ought to act; and I wondered if doctors did, too.

"So I drove out, and on a trash pile next to the old barn, Parnell showed me some large hulls, or pods of some sort, apparently vegetable in origin. Beekey asked me what they were, and I told him the truth, that I didn't know. Well"—Budlong smiled—"he raised his brows at that, as though he was surprised, and since I have my professional pride, it stung me into saying that no botanist alive could identify absolutely anything shown to him. 'Botanist,' young Beekey repeated. Did that mean I thought they were some sort of plant life? And I said yes, I thought they probably were." Budlong shook his head admiringly. "Oh, they're clever, these reporters; they have you making some sort of comment before you quite realize it. Cigarette?" He took a pack from the breast pocket of his coat, and offered Becky one, then me. We shook our heads, and he lighted his own.

"The things he showed me"—Professor Budlong exhaled cigarette smoke—"simply looked to me like very large seed pods, as they'd have looked to anyone,

I'm sure. The old man, Parnell, told me they'd come drifting down from the sky, which I didn't doubt—where else would they come from?—though Parnell seemed amazed. They didn't seem at all remarkable to me, except possibly for their size. Some sort of seed pod was all I could say, though I admitted that the substance they were filled with did not resemble what we ordinarily think of as seeds. Beekey tried to interest me in the fact that several objects in the trash pile on which the pods had fallen seemed very much alike, attributing this fact to the pods. He pointed out two empty Del Monte peaches cans, I remember, which looked identical. There was a broken ax handle, and another similar one beside it. But I couldn't, myself, see anything very startling about that. Then he tried another tack; he wanted a story, you see, a sensational one, if possible, and was determined to get it."

Budlong drew on his cigarette, smiling at us. "Could these things have come, he now wanted to know, from 'outer space,' as he phrased it. Well"—Budlong shrugged—"I could only answer yes, they could have; I simply didn't know where they'd come from. You see"—Professor Budlong sat up in his chair, and leaned forward toward us, forearms on his knees—"this is where young Beekey trapped me. The theory, the notion, whatever you want to call it, that some of our plant life drifted onto this planet from space, is hoary with age. It's a perfectly respectable, reputable theory, and there is nothing sensational or even startling about it. Lord Kelvin—you undoubtedly know this, Doctor—Lord Kelvin, one of the great scientists of modern times, was one of many adherents to this theory, or possibility. Perhaps no life at all began on this planet, he said, but it drifted here through the depths of space. Some spores, he pointed out, have enormous resistance to extremes of cold; and they may have been propelled into the earth's orbit by light pressure. Any student of the subject is familiar with the theory, and there are arguments for and against it.

"So, 'Yes,' I said to the reporter; these could be spores from 'outer space'; why not? I simply didn't know. Well, this seemed astonishing news to my reporter friend, and he joined two of my words as a single phrase. 'Space spores,' he said in a pleased tone, and wrote the phrase on a scrap of paper he was carrying, and I began to see headlines in the making."

Budlong sat back in his chair again. "I should have had better sense, but I'm human; it was fun being interviewed, and in my amusement I amplified the thought, for no other reason than to give young Beekey what he seemed to want." The professor quickly raised his hand. "Not, you understand, that I wasn't speaking the strict truth. It *is* perfectly possible for 'space spores,' if you want to use so dramatic a term, to drift onto the surface of the earth. I think it's quite probable that they have, in fact, though I personally doubt that all life on this planet originated in this way. Advocates of the theory do point out, however, that our planet was once a seething mass of inconceivably hot gas. When finally it cooled to the point at which life was possible, where else could life have come from, they ask, than from outer space?

"In any case, I got carried away." The boyish-looking professor before us grinned. "It's a trait of the academic mind to amplify a theory at great and, quite often, boring length, and standing there on the Parnell farm, I gave the boy his story. Yes, these might be space spores, I said; and equally well, they might be nothing of the kind. In fact, I assured him, I felt quite certain they could be identified, if one were to take the trouble, as something, possibly rare, but perfectly well known, and originating right here on earth in the most commonplace way. The damage was done, however. He chose to print the first portion of my comments, omitting the second, and two or three rather flamboyant and, I felt, misleading newspaper stories, quoting me, appeared in the local paper, which I complained about. And that's the story, Doctor Bennell; much ado about nothing, I'm afraid."

I smiled, matching my mood to his. "'Light pressure,' you said, Professor Budlong. These pods might have been propelled through space by the pressure of light. That interests me."

"Well"—he smiled—"it interested young Beekey, too. And he had me; I'd given him part of the theory, I had to give him the rest. There's nothing mysterious about it, Doctor. Light is energy, as you know, and any object drifting in space, seed pods or anything else, would indisputably be pushed along by the force of light. Light has a very definite, measurable force; it even has weight. The sunlight lying on an acre of farm land weighs several tons, believe it or not. And if seed pods, for example, out in space, lay in the path of light that eventually reaches the earth—the light from distant stars, or any source at all—they would be propelled toward it by the stream of light steadily beating against them."

"Be pretty slow, though, wouldn't it?" I smiled at him.

He nodded. "Infinitely slow, so slow it would hardly be measurable. But what is infinite slowness in infinite time? Once you assume these spores may have drifted in from space, then it is equally true that they may have been out there for millions of years. Hundreds of millions of years; it simply doesn't matter.

A corked bottle tossed into the ocean may circle the globe, given enough time. Expand the speck that is our globe into the immense distances of space, and it is still true that, given enough time, any of these distances may be crossed. So if these, or any spores, drifted to earth, they may well have begun their journey ages before there even was an earth."

He reached forward to tap me on the knee, smiling at Becky. "But you aren't a newspaper reporter, Doctor Bennell. The seed pods on the old Parnell farm, if that is what they were, probably drifted there on the wind, from not too great a distance, and were undoubtedly a completely well-known and classified specimen with which I simply didn't happen to be familiar. And I'm sure I could have avoided a great deal of kidding from my colleagues at the school if I had simply said so to young Beekey. Instead of allowing him to take my theories and make me run with them." He grinned at us again, a very likeable guy.

I sat thinking about what he said, and after a moment he said gently, "Why are you interested, Doctor Bennell?"

"Well—" I hesitated, wondering how much I could, or should, say to him. Then I said, "Have you heard anything, Professor Budlong, about a—sort of delusion that has been occurring here in Mill Valley?"

"Yes, a little." He looked at me wonderingly, then nodded at a mass of papers on the desk before him. "I've been working hard for the past couple months on what I feel, or hope, is a fairly important technical paper scheduled for winter publication; it will mean a great deal to me professionally. And I've been more or less out of circulation, working on it. But a psychology instructor at school did tell me something about an apparent, though temporary, delusion of personality change which several local people have had. You think there's some connection between that, and"—he grinned—"our 'space spores'?"

I glanced at my watch, and stood up; in just over three minutes, Jack Belicec was due to drive down this street, and I wanted us out at the tall hedge in front of the house, ready to step into his car. "Possibly," I answered Professor Budlong. "Tell me this: could these spores conceivably be some sort of weird alien organism with the ability to imitate, in fact, duplicate a human body? Turn themselves, for all practical purposes, into a kind of human being, indistinguishable from the real thing?"

The pleasant-faced, youthful-looking man at the desk before me looked at me curiously, studying my face for a moment. Then, when he spoke, after apparently considering my question, his tone was carefully polite; he was treating an utterly absurd question, for the sake of good manners, with a seriousness it did not deserve. "I'm afraid not, Doctor Bennell. There aren't many things"—he smiled at me—"that you can assert with absolute positiveness, but one of them is this. No substance in the universe could possibly reconstitute itself into the amazing structure of living bone, blood, and infinitely complex cellular organization that is a human being. Or any other living animal. It's impossible; absurd, I'm afraid. Whatever you feel you may have observed, Doctor, you're on the wrong tack. I know myself how easy it is, at times, to be carried away by a theory. But you're a doctor, and when you think about it, you'll know I'm right."

I did know. I felt my face flush in complete confusion, unable to think, and I stood there feeling I'd made the most ridiculous kind of fool of myself, and that of all people, I, a doctor, should have had more sense, and I wanted to drop through the floor, or disappear in thin air. Quickly, almost abruptly, I thanked Budlong, shaking his hand; all I wanted was to get away from this intelligent, pleasant-eyed man whose face was so carefully refraining from showing the contempt he must have felt. A few moments later, he was politely showing us out the front door, and as we walked down the steps toward the wooden gate in the high shrub along the front edge of the lawn, I was grateful to hear the door close behind us.

I wasn't thinking, I was mentally still back in that study feeling like a child who's disgraced himself, and I actually had my hand on the gate latch, fumbling with the mechanism. Then I stopped; a few hundred yards off to our right, I heard a car, moving very fast, swing around the corner and into this street, the rubber squealing on the pavement as though it would never stop. An instant later, through the lattice-work of the gate, I saw Jack Belicec's car flash past, Jack hunched over the wheel, eyes straight ahead, Theodora crouched beside him, the motor roaring. Another set of tires squealed around the corner to the right, out of sight over the high hedge; then, a split second later, a shot sounded, the sharp, unmistakable crack of a gun, and we actually heard the faint, high whistle of the bullet ripping the air of the street before us. A black-and-white gold-starred Mill Valley police car shot past our gate; and then, in an incredibly few moments, the twin sounds of racing motors had diminished, faded, sounded once again very faintly, then they were gone.

Behind us, the front door opened, and now I unlatched the gate, and holding Becky's elbow tightly, I walked with her—quickly, but not running—along the sidewalk, and down two houses. We turned, then, into a walk leading to a two-storied, white clapboard house

I'd played in as a boy. We walked along the side, and through the back yard; behind us, on the street we'd just left, I heard a voice call out, another voice answer, then the slam of a door. A moment later, we were again climbing the hill that rose behind the row of houses, and then, once more, we were hurrying along a path threading through underbrush, occasional eucalyptus and oak trees, and second-growth saplings.

I'd had time to think; I knew what had happened, and I was astounded at the kind of nerve and clear-headed intelligence and thoughtfulness Jack Belicec had shown. There was no telling how long he'd been chased, though it couldn't have been long. But I knew he must have driven through Mill Valley streets, a police car behind him and shooting, with one eye on his watch. Deliberately passing up whatever chances he'd had to escape, to drive out of this town and into the world and safety beyond it, Jack had driven so as to lead the chase closer and closer to the street and home he knew we'd be waiting at, until the minute hand of his watch told him we'd see—just what we had seen. It was the only way he could warn us, and, incredibly, he'd done so, at a time when horror and panic must have been fighting for his mind. And all I could do for him now was hope that somehow he and his wife would escape, and I was certain they could not—that the nearly impassable roads he could drive out on would be blocked now, other police cars waiting and ready for them. And now I knew what a terrible mistake we had made coming back to Mill Valley, how helpless we were against whatever was ruling this town; and I wondered how long it would be—at the next step, the next bend of the path perhaps—before we were caught, and what would happen to us then.

Fear—a stimulant at first, the adrenalin pumping

into the blood stream—is finally exhausting. Becky
was clinging to my arm, unaware of how much of her
weight she was making me carry, and her face was
bloodless, her eyes half closed, her lips parted, and she
was sucking in air through her mouth. We couldn't continue to roam and climb these hills much longer. My leg
movements, I noted, were no longer automatic; the
muscles were responding now only through an effort of
will. Somewhere we had to find sanctuary, and there
was none—not a home at which we dared to appear,
not a face, even that of a lifelong friend, to which we
dared risk appealing for help.

CHAPTER

FIFTEEN

Our main street curves and winds along the foot of a miniature range of hills, as do a great many of the town's streets. We were climbing, presently, down the side of one of these hills, winding along a footpath which would end at the little alley at the back of a block of business buildings, including the building in which I had my office.

It was the best I could think of; all I could think of. I was afraid to go there, but more afraid not to; and in a curious way I thought it was perfectly possible that we might be safe there, for a time, anyway. Because it wasn't a place we could be expected to go to; not until time had passed, and we weren't found anywhere else. And right now, we simply had to have an hour of rest, at least. We might even sleep, I thought, leading Becky down the hill, though I didn't really think we could. But I had benzedrine in the office, and a few other drugs, stimulants that, after an hour's rest to think of some sort of plan, might give us the strength to carry it out.

Below us, now, I could see, over the roofs of the buildings we were approaching, the business street I'd known as long I could remember; the Sequoia, where I'd watched so many Saturday-afternoon movies as a kid; Bennett's Variety Store, where I'd bought candy for the show, and where I'd had a job one high-school summer vacation; and the three-room apartment over one group of stores where I'd been half a dozen times, one summer, my first year in college, calling on a girl who lived there alone.

We reached the alley, and there was no one in it, only a dog sniffing at a refuse-filled carton. We crossed it, and walked into the two-story office building through the open sheet-steel door that led into the white-painted, concrete-block, back stairwell.

I was ready to try and take with us anyone, man or woman, we might have met on those stairs; but we met no one. On the second floor, my ear at the closed metal fire-door, I listened. No sound, and I pulled the door open. We walked silently along the empty hallway to the opaque-glassed door that bore my name. I had my key out and ready, and then we were inside my office, the door clicking shut behind us.

My waiting room and office were already dusty, I saw as I wandered through it, looking the place over; a fine film of dust over every glass and wood surface. My nurse, I knew, wouldn't have been near the place since I'd been here last, and now it smelled unused and closed-in, and was dark, every Venetian blind closed tight. It was quiet and dead, and no longer friendly, as though I'd been away too long and it weren't really mine any more. The place looked untouched, and I didn't bother trying to see if anyone had been here, searching through it for some reason. Right now, I just couldn't care.

There's a long, wide chesterfield in the waiting room, and I put Becky on it, her shoes off. I got a couple sheets, and the pillow from the examining-table, and tucked her in carefully. She lay watching me, not saying anything, and when our eyes met, she smiled wanly, in thanks. Crouching beside her, I took her face in my hands, and kissed her, a gesture of comfort, like kissing a child, no sex in it; she was worn out, at the end of her rope. I passed my hand slowly over her forehead, stroking it. "Sleep," I said. "Get some rest." I smiled and winked at her, looking, I hoped, calm and confident, as though I knew what I was doing, and was going to do.

My shoes off, so no one passing by in the hall outside could hear me, I untied the leather pad from my examining-table, took it out to the waiting room to the row of windows overlooking Throckmorton Street, and laid it on the floor paralleling the windows. Then I un-buttoned my coat, loosened my tie, and sat down. My back against the side wall, I slowly tilted one slat of the Venetian blind just enough to peer down at Throckmor-ton, and now I felt better. Enclosed in these dark, si-lent rooms, I'd felt blind and helpless, but now looking down on the street below, watching the activity on it, I felt more in control of things.

The scene I saw through that quarter-inch slit was ordinary enough at first glance; drive along the main street of any of a hundred thousand American small towns, and you'll be seeing what I did. There were parked cars on an asphalt street, sidewalks and parking meters, white-ruled parking spaces, and people walk-ing in and out of Redhill Liquors, the drug store, Var-ney's Hardware, and a dozen others. There was a little fog, no more than a mist, moving in from the Bay. Throckmorton jogs at the corner just past my windows, and a side street joins it at that corner. So the paved street area is more than usually wide there, and because of the jog in the street, the wide area of pavement is almost completely enclosed on three sides by stores; the nearest thing to a sort of town square we've got. They occasionally set up a bandstand here for street dances or carnivals.

I lay watching, changing position now and then, occasionally lying on my side, propped on an elbow, my eyes just over the window sill; once I lay on my back, staring up at the ceiling. I've long since learned that thinking is mostly an unconscious process: that it's usually best not to force it, particularly when the problem itself is vague in your mind, and you don't really know what sort of answer you're hunting for. So I rested—tired, but not sleepy—watching the street, waiting for something to happen inside my mind.

There's fascination about monotony in motion: the steady flicker of a fire, an endless series of waves slowly crashing on a beach, the unvarying movement of a piece of machinery. And I stared down at the street for minute after minute, watching the shifting patterns that over and over almost, but never quite, repeated themselves: women walking into the market, and women coming out, arms around brown-paper sacks, clutching at purses or children, or both; cars moving out of the parking spaces, others slipping into the white-ruled slots; a mailman moving into and out of one store after another; an old man plodding along; three young boys horsing around.

It all looked so *ordinary;* there were red-and-white paper signs pasted on the windows of the market: advertising Niblets, round steak, bananas, and laundry soap. Varney's hardware store had one window filled with kitchen equipment: pots, pans, electric mixers, irons; and in the other window, power tools. The dime-store windows were loaded with model airplanes and paper cut-out dolls, and staring at the red-and-gold front, I could almost smell that dime-store fragrance. Stretching across the street, near the Sequoia theater, hung a rather faded banner, red with white letters; *Mill Valley Bargain Jubilee*, it read, an annual sale of the merchants. This year, though, it looked as though they hadn't bothered painting a new banner.

Almost directly ahead across the street, a little to the right, I saw the bus from Marin City pull in. Only three people got out: a man and a woman together, and a man with a brown-paper parcel he carried by the string. There was no one waiting to get on the bus, and after a minute or so it pulled out of the beige-and-tan depot into Miller Avenue, heading for the distant free-way, and for some reason it occurred to me—I knew the bus schedules—that there wouldn't be another bus entering or leaving town for the next fifty-one minutes, and that things had changed on the street below me.

It isn't easy to say just how they had changed. The fog was heavier, touching the higher roof tops now, thick and gray, but that was normal, that wasn't the change. There were more people on the street, but... this was the change: they weren't quite acting like a normal Saturday-afternoon-shoppers crowd. Some were still moving in and out of stores, but quite a few of them were just sitting in their cars; some with a door open, feet hooked on the side, talking to the people in the next car; others reading newspapers or fiddling with car radios, just killing time. I recognized a great many of the faces: Len Pearlman, the optometrist, Jim Clark, and his wife, Shirley, and their kids, and so on.

At this moment, though, Throckmorton Street of Mill Valley, California, could still have seemed like an ordinary, though rather shabby shopping street on an ordinary Saturday—it's what a stranger would have thought, driving through town. But looking down at it now, I knew, or at least sensed, that there was more to it than that. There was an atmosphere of . . . something about to happen, a quiet waiting for something expected. It was—I tried to put it into words, sitting there watching through the slit in the blind—like people slowly gathering for a parade. But that wasn't quite it, either. Possibly it was more like a group of soldiers leisurely assembling for some routine formation; some of them talking, smiling, or laughing with others; some reading quietly; others just sitting or standing off by themselves, waiting. I guess the atmosphere down on that street was simply—expectation without any special excitement about it.

Then Bill Bittner, a local contractor, a stout middle-aged man in his fifties strolling along the sidewalk, glancing at store windows, casually pulled a button out of his pocket. It was a plastic or metal button, I could see, with printing on it. He pinned it to his coat lapel, and now I saw that it was about the size of a silver dollar, and I recognized the design and knew what the printing said. It said *Mill Valley Bargain Jubilee;* the local merchants all wore them each year, and passed them out to those customers who were willing to wear them. Only—all those I'd seen before had been red with white printing. Bill Bittner's button was yellow printed on navy blue.

And now, here and there, all up and down the street as far as I could see, other people were pulling out these yellow and blue buttons, and pinning them to their coats. Not everyone did it at once. Most of them just kept on talking, or walking along, or sitting in their cars, or whatever they were doing; and within any half minute, all that a stranger walking along that street would have seen, if he'd even noticed at all, would have been two or three people pinning those buttons to the lapels of their coats. And yet, within five or six minutes perhaps, at one time or another, nearly everyone down there, even Jansek, the parking-meter cop, had brought out a blue-and-yellow *Mill Valley Bargain Jubilee* button and pinned it on in plain sight: some of them even removed red-and-white, otherwise identical, buttons, first.

It took a minute or so, too, to realize this: a gradual movement of people had been going on, from both directions on Throckmorton Street, to the semipublic square below my window. Strolling pedestrians, glancing in windows as they moved, were gradually approaching it; here and there people got casually from their cars, slammed the doors, then stretched, perhaps, or gazed around, or glanced at a window display, then wandered on down toward the square.

Even now, though, a stranger on Throckmorton would probably have seen nothing out of the way. Mill Valley was holding a bargain sale, apparently, and most of the townspeople were wearing Jubilee buttons. At the moment, a considerable number of the shoppers on Throckmorton happened to be crowded into one short block. And yet, all in all, there was nothing out and out strange or remarkable to see.

Becky was kneeling on the floor beside me, I realized, and now I smiled and stood up, to swing the pad on the floor around so that we both could sit on it. I put an arm around her, then, and she huddled close, her cheek next to mine as we both stared down through the Venetian blind.

From the dime store, a salesman walked out to his car; it was lettered on the door with the name of his company. Opening the door, he began hunting for something, apparently, on the floor of the car. Jansek, the cop, glancing at his watch, strolled over, then stopped to stand on the walk beside the front of the car. The salesman straightened, slammed the door of his car, and a sheaf of leaflets in his hand, turned toward the store he'd come out of. Jansek spoke to him, the salesman stepped onto the walk, and they stood there talking. It occurred to me, staring down at them, the salesman facing in our direction now, that he was one of the few people on the street, if there were any others, who was not wearing a blue-and-yellow Jubilee button. He was frowning now, looking bewildered, and Jansek was slowly and firmly shaking his head at whatever the salesman was saying. Then the salesman shrugged irritably, walked around to the driver's side of his car, pulling his keys from his pocket, and Jansek opened the other door and slid into the right-hand front seat. The car backed out, drove ahead a dozen yards, then swung slowly left into the side street, and I knew they were headed for the police station. What Jansek could be arresting him for, I couldn't guess.

A blue Volvo sedan, the only car now moving in the street, drove slowly along in low gear, looking for a space to park. The driver spotted one, then, and began to nose in; the car had Oregon license plates. A cop's whistle sounded, and Beauchamp, the local police sergeant, was trotting down the sidewalk, his paunch jiggling, waving a hand at the car, and shaking his head no. The Oregon car stopped where it was, and the driver sat waiting till Beauchamp came up, the woman beside him leaning forward to peer through the windshield. Beauchamp stooped at the driver's window, they talked for a few moments, then Beauchamp got into the back seat, and the car backed, then pulled ahead, turned left into the side street toward the police station, and disappeared from sight.

There were three more cops in sight, in the nearly two blocks I could see: old Hayes, and two others, younger men I didn't know. Hayes wore a uniform, but the younger men wore uniform caps only, leather jackets, and dark, nondescript pants; they looked like special cops, hired and deputized for a single occasion. Alice, the waitress at Dave's came out and stood on the sidewalk before the door, the blue-and-yellow Jubilee button pinned to her white uniform. One of the younger cops spotted her immediately, and Alice looked at him, nodded her head once, then turned and walked back into the restaurant. The cop came along, then turned into the restaurant.

Maybe a minute later he came out again, and three people, a man, a woman, and an eight- or-nine-year-old girl, obviously a family, were with him. For a moment or so the group stood on the walk, the man talking, protesting about something, the young cop answering politely and patiently. Then the group walked away—toward the side street on which the station house stood—and I watched till they turned the corner and disappeared. None of the family had been wearing a Jubilee button, but the young cop was.

One other man, a delivery-truck driver, got the same treatment; and when he and the cop with him had turned out of sight, there wasn't a soul I could see who wasn't wearing a yellow-and-blue Jubilee button.

And now the street was quiet, almost completely silent, not a car moving or a person walking. No one read a paper, or sat in his car any more. Everyone stood on the sidewalks, three or four deep, facing the street, except Hayes, the old cop, who stood alone in the middle of the wide street. In front of each store or business establishment stood the proprietor, his clerks and employees, and whatever customers had been in the place. Old Hayes, out in the street, slowly turned his head, glancing in turn at each of the proprietors; and each time the proprietor shook his head no. The two other cops, then, came up to Hayes, and reported, apparently, and Hayes listened and nodded. Then, the roll call over, Hayes and the other two cops walked to the sidewalk, turned to face the street, and stood waiting in the crowd.

In two places, looking over roof tops, I could see streets as far as half a mile away. Not a car or anything else moved on any of them, and on one distant street, I could see a barricade across the road: the gray-painted, wooden horses of the street department. I realized suddenly—I knew—that all over town, every street was blocked off like this by crews of men in overalls ostensibly repairing the street. I knew that right now you couldn't get into Mill Valley any way at all, or move along its streets toward the business district. And I knew that the handful of strangers who had happened to be here had been gathered up, and were being held at the police station, under just what pretext it did not matter. Mill Valley was cut off from the world right now, and there was absolutely no one in sight of the center of town who wasn't a resident.

For as long as three or four minutes, then—as strange a sight as I have ever seen—that crowd lined both sidewalks, the street empty, like people watching an invisible parade. They stood almost motionless, and silent; even the children were quiet. Here and there a few men were smoking, but most of the crowd just stood, some of the men with arms folded on their chests, comfortable and relaxed, people occasionally shifting weight from one foot to the other. Children stood holding to their parents' coats.

I heard the motor of a car, then the hood came into sight around the bend of the street, near the Sequoia, a dark-green battered old Chevrolet pickup. Behind it came four other trucks, three of them big GM farm trucks with slatted portable sides, the other another pickup. They drove into the little public square, and parked at the curb, all lined up together. Each of them carried a load covered by canvas tarpaulins, and the drivers, setting their brakes, swung out of the cabs of their trucks, one by one, and began untying the tarps. The scene, now, looked like an open-air market, the produce just arrived from the country. All of the drivers wore overalls of denim pants and shirts, and I knew four of the five. They were all from the few remaining small farms west of town: Joe Grimaldi, Joe Pixley, Art Gessner, Bert Parnell, and one other.

Two men in business suits had stepped into the street, near the line of trucks: Wally Eberhard, a local real-estate man, and another man whose name I couldn't recall, though I remembered he was a mechanic at the Buick garage. Wally had some sheets of paper in his hand, small sheets that looked as though they'd come from a notebook, and the two men stood glancing through them, Wally shuffling them in his hands. Then the mechanic looked up, drew a deep breath, and in a loud voice, almost a shout—we could hear him plainly through our window—called out, "Sausalito! If you have Sausalito families, step out, please!" Sausalito is a Marin County town, the first you come to in the county after crossing the Bay. Two people, a man and a woman, not together, had stepped from the curb into the street and were walking toward

Wally. Several others were pushing their way through the crowd, then they stepped into the street and walked toward the trucks.

Joe Pixley had the tarp on his pickup untied now, and he walked to the back of the truck, took the bottom edge of the tarp, then heaved it up, folding it back onto the truck, off the load. I'd long since known what was in those trucks; I felt not even the beginning of surprise when the tarp came off. Lining the metal sides of the pickup body were thin boards prolonging the height of the sides, and keeping the tarp off the load that was piled cab-high in the truck. It was filled with the huge seed pods I'd seen, now, so often before.

"All right!" the mechanic yelled. "Sausalito! Sausalito only, please!" and he motioned the five or six people standing in the street toward Joe Pixley's truck. Standing on the running board, Joe lifted off the top pods of his load, one by one, handing them down into the waiting arms of the people clustered below him. Each man and woman took a single pod, carrying it away carefully in his outstretched arms; one man took two. Beside them, Wally Eberhard made a check mark on what was apparently a list in his hand, as each pod was handed down. Then he spoke to the mechanic, who called out, "Marin City, please! All with Marin City families or contacts, next!" Marin City is the next Marin County town, a few miles in from Sausalito.

Seven people came forward, five of them black— Marin City has a large black population—edging through the crowd, then stepping into the street, and as they came forward and stopped at his truck, Joe handed down a pod to each. One person, Grace Birk, a middle-aged black woman who worked at the bank, took three, and a man stepped down from the curb to help her carry them without crushing them. I remembered that Grace Birk had a sister and brother-in-law living in Marin City; whether there were more in the family, I didn't know.

The trunk doors of parked cars were being unlocked now, and heaved open; the great pods just fitted into the empty trunks of some of the newer model cars. Other pods were being carefully eased through the open doors of several cars, then set gently down on the back seats. In each case, then, the man or woman, kneeling on the front seat, would place a sheet or some kind of light cloth over the great pod, concealing it from view.

Tiburon was called out next, and eight people came forward for pods, and then Joe Pixley's truck was empty; he sat down on the running board, lighting a cigarette, to wait. The other trucks were uncovered, the drivers standing ready to unload them. The garage mechanic in the neat gray suit called, "Belvedere," and two people stepped out into the street. Corte Madera, Strawberry, Belveron Gardens, and San Rafael were next—fourteen people accepted pods for San Rafael, the largest town of the county. Then every other town in the county was called out, until presently, in no more than fifteen minutes, perhaps, all five trucks were empty, except Joe Grimaldi's, which had two left over.

In less than a minute, then, Wally and the mechanic had stepped into the crowd again, Wally shoving his papers into his inside breast pocket; the crowd itself was shifting and breaking up; the little cavalcade of trucks, starters whirring, motors catching, had backed out into the street, then disappeared down Throckmorton; and all up and down the nearly two blocks we could see, cars with giant pods in their trunks, or concealed in the rear, were pulling out of the parking spaces, then driving away. For a brief time, the crowd, moving along the walks, crossing the street, getting into cars, children darting into and out of it, was heavier than normal, like the sudden glut of people pouring out of a movie after the last show. But it quickly thinned, and I saw women again trundling wire shopping carts inside the market, people sitting down at the counter of Dave's Diner, others sauntering into or out of the various stores. Cars moved slowly along the streets once more. The scene was normal again, a more or less typical main street, perhaps rather more run-down than is usual, but not enough so to arouse wonder in a passing stranger. Not a person in the street wore a yellow-and-blue Jubilee button any more, though one or two wore the red-and-white kind the merchants passed out.

Perhaps five minutes later, I saw the salesman Jansek had arrested driving down Throckmorton, alone in his car, and a few moments after that, the car with Oregon license plates.

My arm still around her, I turned to look at Becky, and she stared at me for a moment, then pursed her lips and shrugged, and I smiled a little in response. There was nothing more to do or say, and I wasn't aware of any particular emotion; certainly there was no new one, and I felt none of the old ones any more strongly. We'd simply reached a limit beyond which there was nothing more to be said or felt.

But I was finally aware—now I knew it for sure —that the entire town of Mill Valley was taken, that not a soul in it but ourselves, and possibly the Belicecs, was what he had been, or what he seemed still, to the naked eye. The men, women, and children in the street and stores below me were something else now, every last one of them. They were each our enemies, including those with the eyes, faces, gestures, and walks of old friends. There was no help for us here, except from each other, and even now the communities around us were being invaded.

CHAPTER

SIXTEEN

W e often say, "I wasn't surprised," or "I knew it would happen"—meaning that in the moment of an event's occurrence, although we'd previously given it no conscious thought, we have a feeling of inevitableness as though we'd known for a long time that precisely this was going to happen. In the minutes we'd been sitting there by the window, all I could think of to do was wait until dark, and then try to work our way through the hills, and out of town; it was useless to try in daylight, with every hand and eye against us. I explained this to Becky, in as hopeful terms as I could, trying to look as though I believed we could succeed; and there were moments when I did feel hopeful.

And yet when I heard the slight grate of a key sliding into the lock of my reception-room door, I had the feeling I've tried to describe. I wasn't surprised; it seemed to me, then, that I'd known all along what would happen, and I even had time to realize that whoever it was had simply gotten the building's master-key from the janitor.

But when the door opened, and I saw the first of the four people who walked into the room, I scrambled to my feet, my heart suddenly elated and pounding. Grinning with wild new hope and excitement, my hand moving out to shake his, I stepped quickly forward, and my voice came out in a harsh, loud whisper. "Mannie!" I said, in a kind of fierce exultation, and I grabbed his hand and shook it.

He responded, though with less vigor than I expected, his hand almost limp in mine, as though accepting but not fully returning my greeting. Then, staring at his face, I knew. It's hard to say how I knew —possibly the eyes lacked a little luster; maybe the muscles of the face had lost just a hint of their usual tension and alertness; and maybe not—but I knew.

Mannie, seeing in my face what was going on in my mind, nodded his head slowly and, as though I'd spoken aloud, said, "Yeah, Miles. And for a long time. Just before the night you phoned me."

I turned to see who else had come into the room, glancing at each face, then I walked back to put my arm around Becky's shoulder, and faced them.

One of the men—they stood there by the door— was small, stout, and bald; I'd never seen him before. Another was Chet Meeker, an accountant in town, a big, black-haired, pleasant-faced man in his middle thirties. The fourth was Budlong, who smiled at us now, as friendly and nice as he'd been before.

We stood by the windows, Becky and I, and Mannie motioned at the chesterfield and said, "Sit down," his voice gentle. We shook our heads, and he repeated it. "Sit down," he urged. "Please, Becky; you're tired, worn out. Go ahead; sit down." But Becky pressed herself closer to me, and I tightened my arm around her shoulders and shook my head again.

"All right." Mannie pushed the sheets on the chesterfield aside and sat down. Chet Meeker walked in and sat beside him, Budlong took a chair across the room from them, and the little man I didn't know sat nearer the outer door.

"I wish you'd relax, and take it easy," Mannie said, brows lifting, smiling at us in frank concern for our comfort. "We're not going to hurt you, and once you understand what we . . . have to do"—he shrugged—"I think maybe you'll accept it, and wonder what all the fuss was about." He sat looking at us, then when we didn't reply or move, he sat back on the chesterfield. "Well, first of all, it doesn't hurt; you'll feel nothing. Becky, I promise you that." He sat nibbling at his lip for a moment, getting what he had to say in order, then he looked up at us again. "And when you wake up, you'll feel just exactly the same. You'll be the same, in every thought, memory, habit, and mannerism, right down to the last little atom of your bodies. There's no difference. None. You *are* just the same." He said it forcefully, convincingly, but for the least fraction of an instant, a hint of disbelief in his own words flickered in his eyes.

"Why bother, then?" I said casually. I had no hope in argument, but I had to say something, it seemed to me. "Just let us alone, then. We'll leave town, and we won't come back."

"Well—" Mannie started to answer, then stopped, and looked at Budlong across the room. "Maybe you ought to explain that, Bud."

"All right." Looking pleased, Budlong settled back in his chair, the professor anticipating the joy of teaching, just as he'd done all his life, undoubtedly.

And I found myself wondering if Mannie weren't right, that actually there was no change, and you were still just the way you always had been.

"You saw what you saw, and you know what you know," Budlong began. "You've seen the . . . pods, for lack of another name; seen them change and prepare themselves; twice you've seen the process almost completed. But why force *you* through the process, when there is, as we say, no final difference at all?" Again, as they had in his home, the finger tips of each hand found those of the other, in academic, professorial gesture, and he smiled at us, a youthful, pleasant-faced man. "It's a good question, but there is an answer, and a simple one. As you surmised, the pods are, in a sense, seed pods, though not in the sense that we know seeds. But in any case, they are living matter, capable, just as are seeds, of enormous and complex growth and development. And they did drift through space, the original ones, anyway, over enormous distances, and through milleniums of time, just as I told you. Though of course"—he smiled in polite apology—"I tried to phrase it in a way to cast doubt over the notion. They live, however; they arrived on this planet by pure chance, but having arrived, they have a function to perform, as natural to them as yours are to you. And that's why you must go through the change; the pods must fulfill their function, their reason for being."

"And what's their function?" I said sarcastically.

Budlong shrugged. "The function of all life, everywhere—to survive." For a moment he stared at me. "Life exists throughout the universe, Doctor Bennell, most scientists know that, and willingly admit it; it has to be true, though we've never before encountered it. But it's there, infinite distances away, in every conceivable and inconceivable form, since it exists under enormously varied conditions. Consider, Doctor, that there are planets and life incalculably older than ours; what happens when an ancient planet finally dies? The life form on it must reckon with and prepare for that fact— to survive."

Budlong sat forward in his chair, staring at me, fascinated by what he was saying. "A planet dies," he repeated, "slowly and over immeasurable ages. The life form on it—slowly and over immeasurable ages—must prepare. Prepare for what? For leaving the planet. To arrive where? And when? There is no answer, but one; which they achieved. It is universal adaptability to *any and all other life forms, under any and all other conditions they might possibly encounter.*"

Budlong grinned at us happily, and sat back in his chair; he was having a fine time. Outside on the street, a car honked, and a child began to wail. "So in a sense, of course, the pods are a parasite on whatever life they encountered," Budlong went on. "But they are the perfect parasite, capable of far more than clinging to the host. They are completely evolved life; they have the ability to re-form and reconstitute themselves into perfect duplication, cell for living cell, of any life form they may encounter in whatever conditions that life has suited itself for."

My face must have shown what I was thinking, because Budlong grinned, and held up a hand. "I know; it sounds like gibbering—insane raving. That's only natural. Because we're trapped by our own conceptions, Doctor, our necessarily limited notions of what life can be. Actually, we can't really conceive of anything very much different from ourselves, and whatever other life exists on this one little planet. Prove it yourself; what do imaginary men from Mars, in our comic strips and fiction, resemble? Think about it.

They resemble grotesque versions of *ourselves*—we can't imagine anything different! Oh, they may have six legs, three arms, and antennae sprouting from their heads"—he smiled—"like insects we're familiar with. But they are nothing fundamentally different from what we know."

He held up a finger, as though reproving an unprepared pupil. "But to accept our own limitations, and really believe that evolution through the universe must, for some reason, follow paths similar to our own, in any least way, is"—he shrugged, and smiled—"rather insular. In fact, downright provincial. Life takes whatever form it must: a monster forty feet high, with an immense neck, and weighing tons—call it a dinosaur. When conditions change, and the dinosaur is no longer possible, it is gone. But life isn't; it's still there, in a new form. *Any form necessary.*" His face was solemn. "The truth is what I say. It did happen. The pods arrived, drifting onto our planet as they have onto others, and they performed, and are now performing their simple and natural function—which is to survive on this planet. And they do so by exercising their evolved ability to adapt and take over and duplicate cell for cell, the life this planet is suited for."

I didn't know what good time would do us. But I was willing—anxious—to talk just as long as he wanted: the will to survive, I supposed, and smiled. "Jargon," I said tauntingly. "Cheap theory. Because *how*; how could they do it? And in any case, how do you know? What do *you* know about other planets and life forms?" I said it jeeringly, nastily, and with a bite in my voice, and I felt Becky's shoulders tremble momentarily, under my arm.

He didn't get mad. "We know," he said simply. "There is"—he shrugged—"not memory; you can't call it that; can't call it anything you could ever recognize. But there is knowledge in this life form, of course, and —it stays. I am still what I was, in every respect, right down to a scar on my foot I got as a child; I am still Bernard Budlong. But the other knowledge is there, too, now. It stays, and I know. We all do."

For a moment he sat staring at nothing, then he looked up at us again. "As to how does it happen, how do they do what they do?" He grinned at me. "Come now, Doctor Bennell; think how little we actually know on this raw, new little planet. We're just out of the trees; still savages! Only two hundred years ago, you doctors didn't even know blood circulated. You thought it was a motionless fluid filling the body like water in a sack. And in my own lifetime, the existence of brain waves wasn't even suspected. Think of it, Doctor! Brain waves, actual electrical emanations from the brain, in specific identifiable patterns, penetrating the skull to the outside, to be picked up, amplified, and charted. You can sit and watch them on a screen. Are you an epileptic, actual or even potential? The pattern of your own individual brain waves will instantly answer that question, as you very well know; you're a doctor. And brain waves have always existed; they weren't invented, only discovered. People have always had them, just as they've always had fingerprints; Abraham Lincoln, Pontius Pilate, and Cro-Magnon man. We just didn't know it, that's all."

He sighed, and said, "And there is a great deal more we don't know or even begin to suspect. Not only your brain, but your entire body, every cell of it emanates waves as individual as fingerprints. Do you believe that, Doctor?" He smiled. "Well, do you believe that utterly invisible, undetectable waves can emanate from a room, move silently through space, be picked up, and then reproduce precisely every word, sound, and tone to be heard in that original room? The sound of a whispered voice, the note of a piano, the plucked string of a guitar? Your grandfather would never have believed such an impossibility, but you do—you believe in radio. You even believe in television."

He nodded. "Yes, Doctor Bennell, your body contains a pattern, all living matter does—it is the very foundation of cellular life. Because it is composed of the tiny electrical force-lines that hold together the very atoms that constitute your being. And therefore it is a pattern—infinitely more perfect and detailed than any blueprint could be—of the precise atomic constitution of your body at exactly that moment, altering with every breath you take, and with every second of time in which your body infinitesimally changes. And it is during sleep, incidentally, when that change occurs least; and during sleep when that pattern can be taken from you, absorbed like static electricity, from one body to another."

Again he nodded. "So it can happen, Doctor Bennell, and rather easily; the intricate pattern of electrical force-lines that knit together every atom of your body to form and constitute every last cell of it—can be slowly transferred. And then, since every kind of atom in the universe is identical—the building blocks of the universe—you are precisely duplicated, atom for atom, molecule for molecule, cell for cell, down to the tiniest scar or hair on your wrist. And what happens to the original? The atoms that formerly composed you are— static now, nothing, a pile of gray fluff. It can happen, does happen, and you know that it *has* happened; and yet you will not accept it." He watched me for a moment, then smiled. "Though perhaps I'm wrong about that; I think maybe you have accepted it."

For a time, then, the room was silent, the four figures in my waiting room quietly watching Becky and me. He was right; I believed him. I *knew* it was true, possible or impossible, and the helplessness and frustration were rising up in me. I could feel it in my finger tips, an actual physical sensation, a compelling urgency to *do* something, and I sat there, my fists clenching and unclenching. Suddenly, impulsively, for no other reason than to move, to act, to do *something*, I reached behind me, grabbed the cord of the Venetian blind, and yanked. The blinds shot up, the slats rattling like machine-gun fire, daylight slanting into the room; and I turned to look down at the wandering shoppers, the stores, the cars, the parking meters, the so ordinary scene below.

The four figures in my office didn't move, just sat watching me; and now my eyes were darting around the room, frantically searching for something I could *do.*

Mannie realized what was going on in my mind before I did. "You could grab something and heave it through the window, Miles. And it would attract attention; people would look up and see the smashed window. You could stand there, then, and shout at them, Miles. But no one would come up." My eyes swung to the phone, and Mannie said, "Grab it; we won't stop you. But you won't get a call through."

Becky's head swung toward me, and she buried her face on my chest, her hands clutching my lapels; and, my arms around her, I felt her shoulders heave in a dry and soundless sob.

"Then what are you *waiting* for!" There was an actual red mist swarming before my eyes. "What are you *doing*, torturing us?"

Mannie grimaced, his face apparently pained, and he was shaking his head. "*No*, Miles! No, we're not. We haven't the least desire to hurt or torture you in any way. You're friends of mine! Or were." He shook his head, hands outspread helplessly. "Don't you see? There's nothing we can *do*, Miles, but wait; and try to explain, make you understand and accept this, try to make this as easy on you as we can. Miles," he said simply, "we have to wait till you're asleep, that's all. And there's no way you can make a man sleep."

Mannie looked at me for a moment, then added gently, "But there's no way you can keep from sleeping, either. You can fight it off for a time, but finally... you'll have to sleep."

The little man near the door—I'd forgotten he existed—sighed, and said, "Lock them in a cell at the jail; they'll sleep eventually. Why all the argument?"

Mannie looked at him coldly. "Because these people are friends of mine. Go on home, if you want to; three of us are enough."

The little man just sighed—no one ever got mad, I noticed—and continued to sit where he was.

Mannie got up suddenly, walked toward us, and stood looking down at me, his face pained and regretful. "Miles, face it. You're caught; there's nothing you can do. Face it, and accept it; do you *like* seeing Becky this way? I don't!" We stared at each other for several ticks of a clock, and somehow I didn't believe in his anguish at all. Gently, persuasively, Mannie said, "Talk to her, Miles. Make her see the truth. No fooling, you won't *mind*, I tell you. You'll feel nothing at all. Sleep, and you'll wake up feeling exactly the same as you do now, only rested. You'll *be* the same. What the hell are you fighting?" After a moment he turned, and walked back to the chesterfield.

CHAPTER

SEVENTEEN

My hand was moving, stroking Becky's hair, gently massaging her neck, comforting her, or trying to, in the only way I could. And then I wondered if it was the only way. I was tired; I could feel it behind my eyes, and in the slackening of my facial muscles; I could feel the weariness of my legs and arms. I wasn't exhausted; I could hold out for a time, but not for too long, nor could Becky. And the idea of sleep, of just dropping my problems and letting go; letting sleep pour through me, and then waking up, feeling just the same as I did now, still Miles Bennell—it was shocking to realize how terribly tempting the idea was.

I looked up at Mannie, sitting there on the edge of the chesterfield, eyes wide, his face looking compassionate and anxious, wanting me to believe him; and I wondered if what he said wasn't the simple truth. Even if it wasn't, holding Becky, feeling the tiny tremble of her body, and knowing how terrified she was, was more than I could take, and I knew there was something more I could do for her than simply sitting there stroking her hair. I could persuade her. I could accept what Mannie had said—accept and *believe* it—and then let my conviction convince her. It might even be true; it *might*.

My hand steadily stroking Becky's hair, holding her tight to me, I thought about it, feeling the steady trembling of her body, feeling my own weariness, letting the will to believe strengthen and grow. Then... Budlong was right; the will to survive cannot be denied—and I knew we'd fight, that we had to. Like a condemned man futilely holding his last breath in a gas chamber, we had to hold out as long as we possibly could, struggling and hoping even when there was no possible hope left. And now I turned to Budlong, trying to think of something, anything, to say, to keep us awake, to find some point of attack, hoping for I didn't know what.

"How did it happen?" I said conversationally. "All of Mill Valley—how did it work?"

He was willing to answer, and I knew Mannie was right: they were simply going to wait, till finally we had to sleep. "A little blindly, at first," Budlong said pleasantly. "The hulls, the pods, drifted down in this area; it could have been anywhere, but it happened to be here. They came to rest on the Parnell farm, on a trash pile, and their first efforts were merely a blind duplication of what they encountered first: an empty tin can stained with the juice of once-living fruit, a broken ax handle of wood. It's a natural waste; the waste of any kind of seed spore falling in the wrong places. Others, though, a few of them—and as a matter of fact, it would have taken only one success—fell, or drifted, or were blown, or carried by curious people, into the right places. And then those who were changed recruited others, usually their own families. The case of your friend, Wilma Lentz, is a typical one; it was her uncle, of course, who placed the hull in their basement that—effected her change. It was Becky's father who—" Politely, he didn't finish that sentence.

"In any event, from the moment the first effective changeover occurred, chance was no longer a factor. One man alone, Charley Bucholtz, the local gas- and electric-meter reader, brought about over seventy changeovers; he enters basements freely, and usually with no one accompanying him. Delivery men, plumbers, carpenters, effected others. And of course once a changeover had occurred in a household, the rest were usually rather easily and quickly made."

He sighed regretfully. "There were accidents, of course; slipups. One woman saw her sister lying in bed, asleep, and a moment later—the process unfinished, as yet—she also saw her sister, apparently, lying asleep in a guest-room closet. She simply lost her mind. Some people, realizing—struggled. They resisted and fought—it's hard to see why—and it was . . . unpleasant for everyone. Households with children were occasionally a little difficult; they're sometimes quick to recognize even tiny and trivial differences. But all in all, it was simple and fast. Your friend, Wilma Lentz, and you, Miss Driscoll, are sensitive people; most people weren't aware of any change at all, because there is none of significance. And of course, the more changeovers made, the more rapidly the remainder go."

And now I'd found a point of attack. "But there is a difference; you just said so."

"Not really, and nothing lasting."

But I wouldn't let it go; he'd reminded me of something. "I saw something in your study," I said slowly, thinking about it. "It meant nothing to me at the time, but now you've made me remember it. And I'm remembering something Wilma Lentz said, too, before she changed." They sat watching, quietly waiting. "You told me in your study that you were working on a thesis, or paper of some sort; a scientific study, and an important one to you."

"Yes."

I leaned toward him, my eyes holding his, and Becky lifted her head, to stare at my face, then turned to Budlong. "There was only one way Wilma Lentz knew Ira wasn't Ira. Just one way to tell, because it was the only difference. There was *no emotion*, not really, not strong and human, but only the memory and pretense of it, in the thing that looked, talked, and acted like Ira in every other way."

My voice dropped. "And there's none in you, Budlong; you can only remember it. There's no real joy, fear, hope, or excitement in you, not any more. You live in the same kind of grayness as the filthy stuff that formed you." I smiled at him. "Professor, there's a look papers get when they're left spread out on a desk for days. They lose their freshness, somehow; they look different; the paper wilts, wrinkles a little from the air and moisture, or I don't know what. But you can tell by looking that they've been there a long time. And that's how yours looked; you haven't touched them since the day, whenever it was, that you stopped being Budlong. Because you don't care any more; they mean nothing to you! Ambition, hope, excitement—you haven't any.

"Mannie"—I swung to him. "The high-school text-book you were planning: *An Introduction to Psychiatry*. The draft you were working on every spare minute you had—what's happened to it, Mannie? When did you last work on it, or even look at it?"

"All right, Miles," he said quietly, "so you know. We tried to make it easy on you, that's all; because after it was over, it wouldn't have mattered, you just wouldn't have cared. Miles, I mean it"—his brows raised persuasively—"it's not so bad. Ambition, excitement— what's so good about them?" he said, and I could tell he meant it. "And do you mean to say you'll miss the strain and worry that goes along with them? It's not bad, Miles, and I mean that. It's peaceful, it's quiet. And food still tastes good, books are still good to read—"

"But not to write," I said quietly. "Not the labor, hope, and struggle of writing them. Or feeling the emotions that make them. That's all gone, isn't it, Mannie?"

He shrugged. "I won't argue with you, Miles. You seem to have guessed pretty well how things are."

"No emotion." I said it aloud, but wonderingly, speaking to myself. "Mannie," I said, as it occurred to me, "can you make love, have children?"

He looked at me for a moment. "I think you know that we can't, Miles. Hell," he said then, and it was as close to anger as he was capable of coming, "you might as well know the truth; you're insisting on it. The duplication *isn't* perfect. And can't be. It's like the artificial compounds nuclear physicists are fooling with: unstable, unable to hold their form. We can't live, Miles. The last of us will be dead"—he gestured with a hand, as though it didn't matter—"in five years at the most."

"And that's not all," I said softly. "It's everything living; not just men, but animals, trees, grass, everything that lives. Isn't that right, Mannie?"

He smiled wryly, tiredly. Then he stood, walked to the windows, and pointed. There, in the afternoon sky, hung a crescent moon, pale and silvery in the daylight, but very clear. A thin streamer of fog was moving across it. "Look at it, Miles—it's dead; there hasn't been a particle of change on its surface since man began studying it. But haven't you ever wondered why the moon is a desert of nothingness? The *moon*, so close to the earth, so very much like it, once even a part of it; why should it be dead?"

He was silent for a moment, and we stared at the silent, unchanging surface of the moon. "Well, it wasn't always," Mannie said softly. "Once it was alive." He turned away, back to the chesterfield. "And the other planets, revolving around the same life-giving sun as this one; Mars, for example." His shoulder lifted slightly. "Traces of the beings that once lived there still survive in the deserts. And now . . . it's the earth's turn. And when all of these planets are used up, it doesn't matter. The spores will move on, back into space again, to drift for—it doesn't matter for how long or to where. Eventually they'll arrive . . . somewhere. Budlong said it: parasites. Parasites of the universe, and they'll be the last and final survivors in it."

"Don't look so shocked, Doctor," Budlong was saying mildly. "After all, what have you people done— with the forests that covered the continent? And the farm lands you've turned into dust? You, too, have used them up, and then . . . moved on. Don't look so shocked."

I could hardly say it. "The world," I whispered. "You're going to spread over the *world?*"

He smiled tolerantly. "What did you think. This county, then the next ones; and presently northern California. Oregon, Washington, the West Coast, finally; it's an accelerating process, ever faster, always more of us, fewer of you. Presently, fairly quickly, the continent. And then—yes, of course, the world."

I whispered it. "But . . . where do they come from, the pods?"

"They grow, of course. We grow them. Always more and more."

I couldn't help it. "The world," I said softly, then I cried out, "But *why?* Oh, my God, *why?*"

If he could have been angry, he would have. But Budlong only shook his head tolerantly. "Doctor, Doctor, you don't learn. You don't seem to take it in. What have I been telling you? What do *you* do, and for what reason? Why do you breath, eat, sleep, make love, and reproduce your kind? Because it's your *function*, your reason for being. There's no other reason, and *none needed.*" Again he shook his head in wonder that I failed to understand. "You look shocked, actually sick, and yet what has the human race done except spread over this planet till it swarms the globe several billion strong? What have you done with this very continent but expand till you fill it? And where are the buffalo who roamed this land before you? Gone. Where is the passenger pigeon, which literally darkened the skies of America in flocks of *billions?* The last one died in a Philadelphia zoo in 1913. Doctor, the function of life is to *live if it can,* and no other motive can ever be allowed to interfere with that. There is no malice involved; did you hate the buffalo? We must continue because we must; can't you understand that?" He smiled at me pleasantly. "It's the nature of the beast."

And so finally I had to accept it, the condemned man finally exhaling, pausing, then sucking death into his lungs because he can't hold out any longer. There was nothing I could do, but this: I could make the last little time left to us as easy as possible on Becky—if we could only spend it alone.

"Mannie"—I looked up at him—"you said we were friends once, that you remember how it was."

"Of course, Miles."

"I don't think you really feel it any more, but if you can still remember anything of how it was, then leave us alone in here. Lock us in my office, and you'll have just the one hall door to guard. But leave us alone now, Mannie; wait in the hall. Give us that much; we can't get away, and you know it. And how can we sleep with you watching us? It'll come faster this way. Lock us in my office, then wait in the hall, Mannie. It's the last chance we'll ever have to know what really being alive is, and maybe you can remember a little of how that was, too."

Mannie looked over at Budlong, and after a moment Budlong nodded, not caring particularly. Then Mannie turned to Chet Meeker, who shrugged; the little man near the door wasn't even asked. "All right, Miles," Mannie said quietly. "No reason we shouldn't." He nodded at the little man by the door, who stood up and went outside to the building hallway. Mannie walked to the heavy wood door leading to my office, turned the key in the lock, then twisted and tugged at the door handle, testing it. He unlocked it again and held it open for Becky and me to walk through.

Slowly it began swinging shut behind us, and just before it closed, I caught a final glimpse of the little man coming back into the reception room from the building hallway, and his body was nearly hidden by the two enormous pods he was carrying in his arms. Then our door clicked shut, the key turned in the lock, and I heard the faint sound of something brushing against the other side of that door—and I knew that those two great pods were lying on the floor now, by that locked door; so very near to us, yet out of our reach.

CHAPTER

EIGHTEEN

I took Becky's arm, holding her hand flat between mine, squeezing it tight between them, and she looked up at me, and managed to smile. I led her to the big leather chair in front of my desk and she sat down, and I sat on the arm, leaning close to her, my arm around her shoulders.

For a little time we were silent, and I sat remembering the night—not long ago, yet very long ago—when Becky had come here to talk about Wilma, and I realized she was wearing the very same dress, silk, long-sleeved, and with a red and gray pattern. I remembered how glad I'd been to see her that night, realizing that even though we'd had only a few high-school dates, I'd never really forgotten her. And now I understood a lot of things I hadn't before. "I love you, Becky," I said, and she looked up at me to smile, then leaned her head back against my arm.

"I love you, Miles."

I heard a tiny sound from the locked door behind us, familiar, yet for an instant I couldn't recognize it; it was the snapping sound a dry, brittle leaf makes. Then I knew what it was, and glanced quickly at Becky, but if she'd heard it, too, she gave no sign.

"I wish we'd been married, Becky. I wish we were married now."

"So do I."

The faint snapping, crackling sound came again from the other side of the door behind us, and then I was on my feet, prowling the little office, hunting for something, anything, that could help us. More than anything I ever wanted before, I wanted another chance; now there *had* to be a way out of this. Remembering to move silently, I opened my desk drawer; there lay prescription pads, blotters, celluloid calendar cards, paper clips, rubber bands, a broken forceps, pencils, two fountain pens, an imitation-bronze letter opener. I picked up the opener, holding it like a dagger, my fist clenched on the handle, and looked at the varnished surface of the heavy wood door to the reception room. Then I opened my hand and let the useless object drop back into the drawer.

There was my instrument cabinet across the room: in which lay rows of stainless steel forceps, scalpels, hypodermic needles, scissors, disinfectants, antiseptics; and I didn't even bother opening the glass doors. There was the little refrigerator: serums, vaccines, antibiotics, and half a quart of stale ginger ale my nurse had left; and I quietly closed the door. There wasn't much else: the office scale, my examining-table, an enameled white wall cabinet of bandages, adhesive tape, iodine, mercurochrome, merthiolate, tongue depressors; there was furniture, rugs, my desk, pictures and diplomas on the wall—there was nothing.

I turned to Becky, my mouth opening to say something, and my heart stopped, then began to pound, and I took two fast steps to her chair, grabbing her shoulders and shaking hard, and her eyes flew open.

"Oh, Miles!—I was asleep." Her eyes opened wide in terror.

In the lower left-hand desk drawer, I found the benzedrine tablets, went to the washroom for a glass of water, then gave Becky one tablet. I looked at the little bottle for a moment, then slipped it into my pocket without taking a tablet; I could hold out for a while yet, and it was best for us to take these alternately, the one keeping the other awake.

And now I sat at my desk, elbows on the glass top, clenched fists under my cheekbones, Becky watching my eyes to be sure I didn't sleep. If there was any way out of this, it was in my mind, not in my feet prowling the office.

Time passed, with an occasional brittle snap from the other side of the closed door before me, and we both heard, and neither of us would glance at that door. I made myself sit where I was, remembering everything I knew about the great pods.

After a time I looked up slowly; in the leather chair, across my desk, Becky sat silently and alertly watching me, her eyes bright now from the benzedrine. Very quietly, both asking her advice and thinking out loud, I said, "Suppose, just *suppose* there was a way— not to escape; there's no way to escape—but to make them take us somewhere else, instead of here." I shrugged—"To the city jail, I guess. Suppose there was a way to do that?"

"What are you thinking of, Miles?"

"I don't know. Nothing, probably. I was thinking of a way to maybe spoil their damn pods; though I'm not even sure we could. But they'd just get more. They'd take us somewhere else, and get more. We wouldn't have accomplished a thing."

"We might gain a little time," Becky said. "Because I doubt if there are more pods at the moment. I think we saw all that were ready." She nodded at the window, and the street below. "I should think they'd have used all they had ready. Maybe the two out there" —she indicated the locked door—"are the last two we saw left, in Joe Grimaldi's truck."

"There are more growing; all we'd have gained is a little reprieve"—I was soundlessly, frustratedly hitting the knuckles of my fist into the palm of my other hand—"and that's not enough, it's no good." I was frowning hard, trying to think clearly. "A little more time isn't what we want to end up with; if there's a way to make them take us out of here, down out of the building, that has to be our chance; there won't be any other."

Becky said, "Do you think you could . . . hit them, knock them out unexpectedly, leaving the building? Like you did Nick Griv—"

I was shaking my head. "We've got to think *real*, Becky; this isn't a movie, and I'm not a movie hero. No, I couldn't possibly handle four men, or maybe even one. I very much doubt that I could handle Mannie, and Chet Meeker could break me in two. Maybe the professor, or the little fat man." I smiled. Then I spoke seriously again. "Hell, I don't even know we could make them take us out of here. Probably not."

"How would we try, though?" She wouldn't give up.

I pointed to the reception-room door. "Right now, if Budlong is right, the things out there are—preparing. Preparing, more or less blindly at first, to imitate, and duplicate whatever life-substance they encounter; cell and tissue, bone structure, and blood. And that means us—once we lie quietly asleep, our body processes slowed down and defenseless. But suppose—" I looked at Becky, hesitating; if this weren't the answer, I didn't know what else could be. "Suppose," I said slowly, "that we made those two pods out there expend themselves on something else. Suppose we provided a substitute: Fred and his girl friend."

She frowned a little, not getting what I meant, and I reached out and opened the wall closet beside my desk. "The skeletons," I said, pointing at them, standing hollow-eyed and grinning in my closet. "They *did* live." Suddenly I was talking rapidly and excitedly, almost as though convincing Becky were all I need do. "They're bone structure, human, and absolutely complete! And if Budlong is right, the atoms that compose them are held together still, by the very same sort of patterns of force-lines, or whatever he wants to call them, that held them together in life, and that hold ours together now. There they are—asleep and more than asleep! Ready, willing, and just possibly able, to be taken over, their patterns blindly copied and reproduced instead of ours!"

After a moment, Becky said, "We can't lose by trying, Miles," and before she finished, I was on my feet.

In absolute silence, infinitely careful not to bump the loose-swinging limbs against the closet walls, I lifted out, first, the taller male skeleton, carried it to the locked reception-room door, and laid it on the floor, face down so we wouldn't see that grinning face. Seconds later I laid the female skeleton beside it.

We stood looking down at them for a moment, then I turned to the instrument cabinet at the wall, carefully opened the glass door, and took out a 20 cc. syringe. I tilted a glass alcohol dispenser against a wad of sterile cotton, then swabbed a small area on Becky's arm, then on mine, then led Becky to the reception-room door. From a vein in her forearm I withdrew 20 cc. of blood, and a moment later—quickly, before the blood could clot—the collar and several rib bones of the nearer figure on the floor were streaked red. From my own arm I withdrew another 20 cc., and bent quickly over the other figure.

"Miles, don't; *don't.*"

I looked up to see Becky quickly shaking her head, eyes averted, her face paling, but I didn't stop.

"Miles, *please;* I can't stand it; the way they look; *please don't.* No more!"

I stood and turned toward her. "All right"—I nodded. "I don't know at all that it'd do any good, except that it's just that much more living matt—" I let it go and didn't finish. But I left the figures on the floor as they were. I didn't really know what I was doing, but—I left them as they were.

I did one more thing, and didn't ask Becky's permission. I took my desk scissors, snipped off a good chunk of her hair, then a handful of mine, and scattered them on the two figures on the floor. Now there was nothing to do but wait.

We sat, Becky in the leather chair, I at my desk; then Becky began speaking. Slowly, doubtfully, and pausing often to look at me questioningly, she described an idea that had occurred to her.

I listened, and when she stopped, waiting for an answer from me, I smiled and nodded a little, trying not to look immediately discouraging. "Becky, it might—it probably would—work, as far as it goes. But I'd still end up, struggling on a floor, with two or three men on top of me."

She said, "Miles, I know there's no reason why anything we can think of has to work out at all. But now *you're* thinking like a movie. Most people do—sometimes, anyway. Miles, there are certain activities most people never actually encounter all of their lives, so they picture them in terms of movie-like scenes. It's the only source most people have for visualizing things they've had no actual experience of. And that's how you're thinking now: a scene in which you're struggling with two or three men, and—Miles, what am I doing in that scene in your mind? You're seeing me cowering against a wall, eyes wide and frightened, my hands raised to my face in horror, aren't you?"

I thought about it, and she was right, very accurate, in fact, and I nodded.

She nodded, too. "And that's how they'll think: the stereotype of a woman's role in that kind of situation. And it's exactly what I *will* do—until I know they've seen and noticed me. Then I can do exactly what you did; why not?"

I was considering what she'd said, and Becky persisted, unable to wait. "Why *not*, Miles; why can't I?" She paused for an instant, then said, "I can. You'll be beaten up, you'll have a bad minute or so, but then . . . Miles, why couldn't it work?"

I was afraid. I didn't like this at all; this was real, genuinely and simply a matter of life or death for us, and I saw that we were going at it in a spur-of-the-moment, improvising way. We had to *think*, be certain, and make sure of what we were doing—take the time to be right, and know we were right. Yet now, like soldiers suddenly caught in enemy fire, the most important thinking of our lives had to be improvised on the spot under terrible strain, with the penalty for anything less than perfection being death or worse. There was no *time* for more careful planning! We certainly couldn't sleep on it, I thought, and smiled with no amusement at the joke.

"Miles, come *on!*" Becky whispered. She was standing, reaching across the desk, yanking at my sleeve. "You don't know how much longer we have!"

There was a light tapping at the outer door of my office, and from the hallway outside I heard Mannie's voice, very soft and quiet. "Miles?" he whispered, then paused. "Miles . . . ?"

"I'm sorry, Mannie," I called out, "but we're still awake. I can't help that; you know we'll stay awake as long as we can. But it won't be too long; it can't be."

He didn't answer, and now there was no guessing how much longer we'd be alone. I hated what we were going to do, hated pinning hope on this one flimsy notion of Becky's, but certainly I couldn't think of anything else at all. "All right." I stood up, then walked to the little wall cabinet and took out a wide roll of adhesive tape. At the instrument cabinet I gathered up everything else we needed; then, at my desk, I unbuttoned Becky's sleeves at her wrists, pushed back my coat sleeves, and went to work.

It didn't take long, four minutes, maybe, and while I was pulling down my sleeves, Becky buttoning the sleeves of her dress, she gestured with her head—"Miles, look."

I turned to look, narrowed my eyes to make sure I was seeing it, and then I knew I was. The yellow-white bones on the floor looked—different. I can't say how, but, looking at them now, there was simply no doubt that they'd changed.

It may have been the color, though I couldn't be sure, but it was more than that, too. The sense of sight is more subtle than we're accustomed to think; it sees more than we credit it for. We say, "I could tell by looking," and though sometimes we can't explain how that could be, it is usually true. Those bones had lost *hardness*, although I don't even quite know what I mean by that, or how we could see it. Their form hadn't changed, but—they'd lost some degree of rigidity or firmness. Like an ancient wall of loosened bricks, its form still unchanged to the eye, but the mortar crumbling, some strength had left them. Whatever was holding each bone together, giving it its form and shape, was weakening. And the eye could tell it.

Trying not to hope too much, ready for disappointment, not yet able to trust what my eyes saw, I stared. Then suddenly, in the flick of an eye, on a little inch-long segment of the ulna, one of the two bones of the forearm, in the nearest figure on the floor, a patch of gray appeared. Nothing more happened for the beat of a heart; then the patch lengthened, and continued to lengthen, extending in both directions, shooting out along the yellow-white bone. And then—it was like an animated-cartoon sequence in which a picture is sketched impossibly fast, the lines flashing out in all directions faster than the eye can follow. On both figures on the floor under our eyes the gray shot out along the bones, following their lines with enormous speed— the entire rib cage of one in the flash of an eye. Then the bone-whiteness was gone, and for a suspended instant of time the two skeletons lay there composed—in perfect completeness—of a gray weightless fluff. The instant ended, and they collapsed—a puff of air would have done it—into a formless little heap of dust and nothingness on the floor.

For an instant longer I stood staring, wild with elation; then the breath sucked into my lungs, and I yelled out, "Mannie!"

The hallway door of my office opened instantly, and they came in—hurrying—their faces utterly calm and composed. I pointed with the toe of my shoe, and they stopped, stared for a moment, then Mannie pulled the key from his pocket and unlocked the door to my reception room. He opened it, and it bumped something, something hard that clicked on the wood of the door. Mannie pushed, the door opened a little more, then jammed. Then each of us, as fast as we could, moving one at a time, sidled around that partly blocked door.

There on the brown rug, yellow-white and reproduced down to the last useless detail, lay two skeletons, red-daubed on the shoulders, a handful of dark hair filtering through their bones. Face down on the floor, they grinned liplessly and unceasingly at the joke. Beside and under them, nearly unnoticeable on the rug, lay the brittle fragments of all that remained of the two great pods.

Mannie nodded slowly several times, lips folded in, thinking to himself, and Budlong said, "That's very interesting, really very interesting. Do you know"—he turned to me conversationally, eyes friendly as ever—"that had never occurred to me, and yet of course it's perfectly possible. Interesting." He turned to look down at the floor again.

"All right, Miles"—Mannie looked musingly at me—"I guess we will, at that, have to hold you in a cell, till we can get others. Sorry, but it's what we'll have to do."

I just nodded, and we all moved out then, through the door to the building hallway. We walked along the hall to the metal fire-door, then began filing down the staircase.

CHAPTER

NINETEEN

They had Chet Meeker and the little stout man first. Becky and I were in the middle, Mannie and Budlong directly behind us. There was no reason I could think of for waiting, and as we approached the between-floors landing, I brought my hands together, arms hanging loosely before me, and the thumb and forefinger of my left hand reached into my right sleeve, thumb and forefinger of the other hand into the left sleeve. The fingers of each hand touched and pulled loose the strips of adhesive just above my cuff lines. Then—this was Becky's plan—each hand held a loaded hypodermic syringe.

Stepping onto the landing, beginning the half-circle turn, the little stout man was on the inside, gripping the stair rail, and Chet Meeker swung out to walk beside him. I stepped suddenly forward, directly behind them, shoving Becky to one side with an elbow, flinging her into a corner of the landing; both my hands shot instantly forward, hard and fast, the needles clenched tight between my fingers, thumbs on the depressors, and I gave each man 2 cc. of morphine in the great muscles of the buttocks, and plunged the depressors home.

They yelped and swung toward me as Mannie and Budlong crashed onto my back, and I was smashed to the steel floor, gouging, kicking, and stabbing out with my needles. But four against one had me in seconds, one needle kicked out of my hand, the other ground to powder and glass fragments under a heel. They had an arm and both legs pinned tight, and I was wrenching and jerking the free arm, trying to keep them from pinning it. Becky—I saw it, and so did they—stood huddled in a corner against the white concrete-brick walls, trying to keep clear of the struggling mass of men, the flying feet and arms; and she cowered helplessly, eyes wide and frightened, both hands raised in a gesture of horror to her open mouth. Then, as I struggled, the sound of our panting and grunts loud and echoing, Becky's fingers—her hands still upraised, eyes still wide and astonished—flickered at the sleeves of her dress, and the buttons were open. She yanked both strips of adhesive loose, stepped forward suddenly, as Budlong and Mannie leaned over me grabbing at my flailing arm, and plunged both needles home. The two men straightened. I lay there motionless, staring and fascinated, and for a moment we all stood, knelt, or lay in a frozen tableau. They stared at Becky, then looked down at me. "What are you doing?" Budlong said puzzledly. "I don't understand." Then I rolled to my knees, starting to rise, and they were on me again.

It isn't easy to judge how long we struggled there. But then Chet Meeker, kneeling on my arm, sighed gently and toppled limply sideways onto the stairs and rolled, slowly bumping each step, till his feet caught in the stair rail, and he lay there stirring sluggishly and staring up at us. They stared after him, and Mannie said, "Hey." Then the little stout man, kneeling at my head, directly in back of me, hands on my jaws, let go and dropped back, slumping against the wall in a sitting position, and sat there blinking at us.

Budlong looked down at me, his mouth opened to speak, then his knees bent and he sat down hard enough to make the steel floor throb, then he lay down on his side, muttering something I couldn't make out. Mannie had grabbed the thin tubular steel railing with both hands, and now he bent over to lay his forehead on the backs of his clenched hands. After a few moments he slowly knelt to the floor, then his head dropped to hang for a moment between his still clinging arms; then his hands loosened their grip and, still kneeling, he lay face downward on the corrugated metal floor, like a man salaaming.

We ran, not too fast; I kept aware that it was possible to slip and break a bone. Then we were at the metal back door of the building, pushing against it.

It wouldn't open; it was locked, the building empty, and full of weekend silence. And there was simply nothing to do but turn, walk the length of the building lobby, past the wall directory, toward the doors that opened onto Throckmorton Street. I remembered to say to Becky, "Keep your eyes a little wide and blank, not much expression on your face; but don't overdo it." Then I pushed open the doors, and we stepped onto the street, out among the people of dead and forsaken Mill Valley.

Within five steps we passed a man, my age; I'd known him in high school and, my face uninterested and uncaring, I simply nodded, letting my eyes pass over his face in dull recognition. He nodded in the same way, and then we had passed him; I felt Becky's arm, under mine, trembling. We passed a short, plump little woman, carrying a shopping bag, who didn't glance at us. Half a dozen yards ahead, a man slid out of the front seat of a parked car and stood waiting for us, a man in uniform, a policeman, Sam Pink.

I didn't let us break stride or hesitate, and we walked up to him and stopped. "Well, Sam," I said dully, "now we're with you, and it's not so bad." He nodded, but frowningly, and glanced into his car at the humming radio. "They were supposed to let us know," he said. "Kaufman was supposed to phone the station, then we'd get a call."

"I know"—I nodded. "He phoned, but the line was busy; they're calling again now." I turned to gesture with my head at my office building behind us.

Sam was no less and no more bright or quick than he ever had been, and now he stood staring at me, turning over in his mind what I'd said. I waited, uninterested; a moment passed, and then as though I took his silence for the conversation's conclusion, I nodded. "See you Sam," I said emptily and, Becky's arm tight under mine, walked on.

We didn't look back, and we neither increased nor decreased our pace. We walked to the next corner, then turned right. As we turned, I saw Sam Pink turn into the office building and disappear from sight.

And now we ran—down the dead-end half block of small homes that ended in the low range of hills more or less paralleling Throckmorton. Halfway there, a woman stepped out from the walk leading to one of the houses and confronted us, a little old woman who held up her hand in the abrupt, peremptory manner with which old people sometimes halt traffic in order to stroll

across the street. Habit rules us, and I stopped, knowing that this little old lady—a Mrs. Worth, a widow; I
recognized her now—was no little old lady at all, and
that I ought to smash her to the ground with my fist, not
even breaking stride. But I couldn't; she looked like a
woman, old, tiny, and frail, and for a moment I just
stood there, staring at her. Then, suddenly, I brushed
her aside, pushed her with my outflung forearm, and
she staggered back and nearly fell.

Then we were at the end of the concrete walk, our
feet hitting red dirt, and an instant later we were
climbing, turning onto one of the packed-dirt paths that
wound up and through the Marin County hills, and we
were hidden from the street by the straggling under-
growth and wild, tangled shrubbery.

Becky lost her shoes—slippers—in the first
dozen steps, and though I knew what the path, the pebbles, twigs, exposed rocks and roots were doing, and
would do, to her feet, we couldn't stop.

We had no chance; the string was nearly played
out, and I knew it, and didn't try to fool myself about it.
I knew these paths, hills, and winding roadways, every
foot of them, but so did others, plenty of others. And
between us and freeway 101—the passing cars and
humanity from outside—lay perhaps a couple of miles
of hills, paths, fields, and even a last few acres of farm
land. Against any kind of search and pursuit at all, we
couldn't get through, and even as I was thinking so, the
town fire signal began blasting the air, sounding very
close, the fire station only two blocks away in a straight
line. Mill Valley uses, not a siren, but a hoarse, deep-
voiced air-blast signal; in timbre and pitch it's the note
of a foghorn, but the deep notes are short, emitted
quickly in a rapid series of growls that vibrate the air
for miles, penetrating everything. The unending, iden-

tical blasts of sound filled the air and our ears, building a terrible sense of panicky excitement, and I realized that it could make us lose our heads, so that we simply ran blindly and hopelessly.

I knew that men were already flinging themselves into cars, that starters were grinding, motors catching, cars lurching forward, carrying men after us and ahead of us; more and more with every blast of that deep and terrible sound. Far ahead, men were leaving houses to spread through these hills, hunting or waiting for us. The next few minutes—no more than five, perhaps— were the last moments left in which we could even hope to stay unobserved.

Higher on the hill sloping up to our right, the underbrush dwindled and gave place to an open, exposed, useless stretch of field, waist high with brown, fall weeds. Walking in that field, or any of several others like it ahead, we'd be instantly visible to the first man or men to come over the hill's crest or step out from the underbrush below it. Yet to continue walking this path could only mean stepping into the arms of the men who would be prowling it, and every other, within minutes.

Holding Becky by the arm, I stopped and stood in a panic of confused indecision, trying to make one of two hopeless choices. If it were only dark, we wouldn't be limited by the paths; the area of search would be expanded, and— But it was bright daylight, foggy still, but with wide patches of sunlight. Full darkness was several hours off.

I turned suddenly, leading Becky off the path, climbing the hill to the beginning edge of the exposed, momentarily sunlit field of weeds that curved on up to the crest. Stooping, my arms moving fast, I began yanking great handfuls of weeds loose, snapping their brittle stems, gesturing violently at Becky to do the same. Then we had, each of us, a huge armload of weeds, like sheaves of wheat. "Walk ahead," I said to Becky, "out in the field," and without questioning me, she moved, her body pushing through the weeds, leaving a swath, a trail of bent weeds behind her. I followed, walking sideways, sliding along, and with my free arm moving in a steady, scythe-like sweep, I caught up the weeds we'd bent down, straightening them again as I walked. I moved fast, working with desperate carefulness, sweeping the bent weeds to an upright position again. When we'd gone twenty yards, I could see no visible trail behind us.

In the center of the field now, I had Becky lie down, then I lay down beside her. I scattered her armload of yellow weeds over us, covering us; then, as well as I could, I straightened the weeds around us, and set those I carried upright on top of us, spreading them apart till they stood—leaning, sagging in places—but held up by each other in more or less vertical position.

Exactly what it would look like to an observer on the edge of the field, I didn't know; but with no trail leading to it, I could only hope it wouldn't be particularly noticeable. Lying in the middle of a wide and exposed field, apparently searchable at a glance, was, I hoped, a hiding place that wouldn't occur to whoever passed it; a hunter, I told myself, expects the fugitive to run.

Several minutes passed; then—very close, it seemed—I heard a voice call out. I couldn't understand it, quite, but it seemed to be a name—Al, maybe—and another voice answered, "Yeah." I heard the crackling of underbrush; it continued for a time, then faded away, and I reached carefully for Becky's hand and held it.

CHAPTER

TWENTY

We lay for a long time—motionless, terribly uncomfortable at first, then painfully uncomfortable, but never moving, never changing position. From time to time, we heard voices: on the path near us and from farther away. Once, for a long, long time it seemed, though it was probably no more than three to four minutes, we heard two men talking quietly, slowly climbing our hill, cutting through the field we lay in. The voices drew nearer, steadily louder in volume as they approached; then they passed us, no more than thirty yards away. We could have heard clearly, I suppose, what they were saying, but I was too frightened and intent on guessing their progress to pay attention to the sense of their talk. Several times, very distantly, we heard automobile horns, series of short and long blasts in some sort of signal.

Then, after a very long time, we were cold, the damp and chill rising from the ground underneath us, and I knew the sun was low, that time had passed, and that we weren't going to be found, at least not here where we lay.

I forced us, Becky not questioning me, to lie here till full dark, and for the last long spell of it we lay steadily shivering, bone cold, and I had to clench my teeth till my jaws ached painfully, to prevent my teeth from actually chattering.

Finally we stood—stiffly, hardly able to stumble to our feet—and I saw that with darkness there had come advantages. We couldn't be seen now—it was very dark—from even eight or ten yards away, and broken stretches of fog, a real help, drifted low in the sky and across the ground. But there was that crescent moon overhead, and I knew that long before we could walk to the freeway, there would be times when we could be seen clearly. And long since, I knew, in the time we'd lain silent and motionless in this field, the search would have been organized, the hunting party completed; every able-bodied man, woman, and half-grown child in Mill Valley, for all I knew. And there was only one way we could come, the way we now began walking: toward 101. And they knew that, all of them, as well as we.

We weren't going to get out; that was certain, and I understood it. We could only take every least chance we could give ourselves, not giving up, yielding nothing, fighting to the very last instant of time we had left.

We each wore one of my shoes; Becky couldn't keep both of them on, they were far too large. But with a handkerchief stuffed in the heel of the one she wore, she could keep from losing it, dragging it shuffling through the weeds or underbrush, lifting it carefully. Favoring our stockinged feet, we walked on through the dark as quietly as we could, Becky holding my arm,

while I guided us by the shapes of hill crests, an occasional small landmark, and simple dead reckoning.

An hour passed and we'd come over a mile, encountering no one, hearing no one. An illusion of hope
began to grow in me, and I pictured in my mind, like a
map, what lay ahead of us. And—I couldn't help this
—I began visualizing a picture of ourselves reaching
the highway and running across it, stopping traffic suddenly, bunching it up, brakes squealing, twenty or a
hundred cars deep, bumper to bumper, and filled with
real and living people.

We kept on, covering another half mile in another
half hour. Then we were moving down the gentle slope
of the final hill, toward the wide strip of empty land
that paralleled the freeway along the shallow little valley through which it ran. A dozen steps more, and now,
as it had been doing intermittently for an hour, the
moon broke through a gap in the low layers of moving
fog. In the little valley at our feet we could see the
fences, some from the days when this had been farmed,
and, a little to the left, the dark shape of a horse barn;
riding horses were stabled and pastured here. In an
adjoining field, almost flat—it had been graded once
—I saw something I'd never seen before. Between paralleling rows of what appeared to be tiled irrigation
ditches lay row after row of . . . cabbages, perhaps, or
pumpkins, though neither were grown here, not in this
area, nor anything else that I'd ever seen. Fairly round
spheres, dark circular blobs in the faint moonlight,
growing in long, evenly spaced rows. I knew what they
were then, and Becky, beside me, drew in a sudden
sharp breath. There lay the new pods, as large already
as bushel baskets, and still growing; hundreds of them,
in the dim, even light of the moon.

The sight scared me, terrified me, and I hated to

go on, to walk down there and through them, hated the thought of even brushing against one. But we had to, and we sat down, waiting till the fog once more drifted over the face of the moon.

Presently it did; the light dimmed and diminished, but not enough. I wanted to cross this open field in as near to pitch darkness as this night would give us, and we sat there on the dark hillside waiting.

I was very, very tired, and sat slumped, staring dully down at the ground, waiting till it should darken completely. The field below, in which the pods lay, was narrow; perhaps a hundred feet across, no more. Then an acres-wide belt of weeds began, sheltering the pods from the view of the freeway beyond.

I realized, suddenly, what would happen; now I understood why we'd gotten as far as we had, encountering no one. There had been no point in scattering their strength through the territory we had crossed, trying to find us in the darkness. Instead, they were simply waiting for us; hundreds of silent figures strung along together in a solid line hidden in the weed-grown fields between us and the freeway we had to approach, until presently we walked into their waiting arms and hands.

But I told myself this: there is always a chance. Men have escaped from the most tightly guarded prisons other men could contrive. War prisoners have walked hundreds of miles through a population of millions, every one of them his enemy. Sheer luck, a momentary gap in the line at just the right instant, a mistake in identity made in the darkness—until the very moment you are caught, there is always a chance.

And then I saw that we didn't dare take even what little chance we might have had. A low swirl of fog edged off the face of the moon, and again I saw the pods, row after row of them, lying evil and motionless at our feet. If we were caught, what about these pods? We had no right to waste ourselves! We were here—with the pods—and even though it was hopeless, even though it made capture an absolute certainty, we had to use ourselves against the pods. If there was any luck to be had, *this* was how it had to be used.

A minute passed before the first edge of the next wide bank of fog bit into the face of the moon. It covered it slowly, the light dimming, and then, once again, it was full dark, and we stood, and walked silently down the hill, into the monstrous field below us. In it, at one edge, stood a little shed, and we hurried to it, occasionally brushing the dry, brittle surfaces of the great pods, stepping over the ditches between the rows.

In the shed, with the mini-tractor that had scraped out these rows and ditches, I found the tractor gas just inside the open door, six great metal drums of it lined up along the wall on the dirt-packed floor, and the excitement flared up in me, and strength pulsed with my blood through my veins. This was futile, of course; there were hundreds of pods. But the chance to make a stand had to be taken. I shook two benzedrine tablets into Becky's hand, took a couple myself, and we choked them down. Then Becky helped me heave the first drum onto its side. It took me ten minutes, prowling that little shed, lighting one match after another, to find the rusted wrench up on one of the low rafters. Then we rocked the big metal drum, got it rolling, and trundled it out through the door and down to the nearest of the irrigation ditches. The drum in position, the hexagonal metal plug over the lip of the tile, I started the plug with the wrench, then turned it loose with my hand, the gasoline spurting through my fingers. Then the plug dropped out, and in a steady, rhythmic gurgle the gasoline poured into the tiled ditch and began to flow sluggishly. I wedged the drum in place with a clod of dirt, and left it.

Presently six drums of low-test farm gasoline lay side by side at the head of the irrigation ditches, and the first one was already empty. Ten minutes passed; we simply sat there, silently. Then the flow from the last of the drums ceased, except for a slow dripping sound, and I knelt beside the open ditch, the sharp reek of gasoline stinging at my eyes. I lit a match, dropped it into the still slow-flowing pool, and it promptly went out. I lit another, and this time brought it slowly down, till the bottom edge of flame touched the shiny surface; I could see my face reflected in the pool. The flame caught, a little flicker of blue that grew into a circle, half-dollar size for a moment, then swelling to the shape and diameter of a saucer. And then it flared, puffed up smokily so that I jerked my head back, and the flame—red spikes mixing with the blue now— moved down the tiled ditch, widening to its edges, and in another instant it began to race.

The heat grew and multiplied on itself, the flames began to sound—a liquid crackle—and they reddened and shot suddenly high, and the black smoke began to roll. Standing now, we followed the line of flame with our eyes, watched it climbing in height, running down that field in parallel lines, shooting down connecting ditches with a subdued roaring sound, and the black silhouettes of the pods were suddenly sharp against the smoky red flame. The first pod burst into a round torch of pale, almost incandescent flame, the smoke white; then the second, then the fourth and fifth together, then the third. And now the soft, explosive puffs of pods bursting into flame came steady as a clock tick, one after another down the rows, flaring into mushrooming incandescence, and the sudden sound of hundreds of voices moving toward us through the weeds beyond them washed at our ears like surf.

For perhaps a minute I thought we had won, and then of course the gasoline—only six drums of it flowing into the field—burned out. One after another, the racing red lines of flame slowed and stopped, dwindling, at all the points where the last trickles of gasoline had flowed into the ground. The rows of burning torches still glowed, but the flames were redder, the white smoke increasing, and no new ones were catching. The flames—higher than a man at their peak—were suddenly only waist-high, sinking rapidly, and the red lines of fire, once solid and bright, were broken. At almost the same moment, the flames, covering perhaps half an acre of field, subsided to flickering inch-high tongues—and the hundreds of advancing figures were upon us.

They hardly touched us; there was no anger, no emotion in them. Stan Morley, the jeweler, simply laid a hand loosely on my arm, and Ben Ketchel stood beside Becky, in case she should try to run, while the others, gathering around us, looked at us without curiosity.

The two of us, then, in the midst of a straggling mob of hundreds of people, began slowly climbing the hill we'd come down. No one held us, there was very little talk, no excitement; we simply plodded, all of us, on up that hill. One arm around Becky's waist, my other hand on her elbow, I helped her as well as I could, my eyes on the ground, thinking of nothing, feeling nothing, except how tired I was.

And then—the vast low murmur of hundreds of voices all around us sounded again, and I lifted my head. Even as I looked, the murmur stopped abruptly, and I saw that everyone had stopped; they stood stock still, facing the little valley we'd climbed from, and their faces were raised to the sky in the moonlight.

Now I followed their gaze, and in the clear, thin light of the moon I saw what they'd seen. The sky above us was peppered with dots. More than dots; a great awesome swarm of dark, circular blobs drifted, ascending slowly and steadily into the sky. A last trail of mist left the face of the moon, the sky brightened, and I watched the great pods, the field they had come from almost empty now, steadily rising. Then the last few of the pods still on the ground actually moved, leaning to one side to snap the brittle stems that held them. Then they, too, rose with the others, and we watched the great swarm, slowly diminishing in size, never touching or bumping, climbing steadily higher and higher into the sky and the spaces beyond it.

CHAPTER
TWENTY-ONE

Revelation is the word for a complex of thought revealing itself instantaneously with the enormous impact of absolute truth. Standing motionless with Becky, my mouth agape, head far back, staring up at that incredible sight in the night sky, I knew a thousand things it would take minutes to explain, and others I can never explain in a lifetime.

Quite simply, the great pods were leaving a fierce and inhospitable planet. I knew it utterly and a wave of exultation so violent it left me trembling swept through my body; because I knew Becky and I had played our part in what was now happening. We hadn't, and couldn't possibly have been—I saw this now—the only souls who had stumbled and blundered onto what had been happening in Mill Valley. There'd been others, of course, individuals, and little groups, who had done what we had—who had simply refused to give up. Many had lost, but some of us who had not been caught and trapped without a chance had fought implacably, and a fragment of a wartime speech moved through my mind: *We shall fight them in the fields, and in the streets, we shall fight in the hills; we shall never surrender.* True then for one people, it was true always for the whole human race, and now I felt that nothing in the whole vast universe could ever defeat us.

Did this incredible alien life form "think" this, too, or "know" it? Probably not, I thought, or anything our minds could conceive. But it had sensed it; it could tell with certainty that this planet, this little race, would never receive them, would never yield. And Becky and I, in refusing to surrender, but instead fighting their invasion to the end, giving up hope of escape in order to destroy even a few of them, had provided the final conclusive demonstration of that truth. And so now, to *survive*—their one purpose and function—the great pods lifted and rose, climbing up through the faint mist, on and out toward the space they had come from, leaving a fiercely implacable planet behind, to move aimlessly on once again, forever, or . . . it didn't matter.

I don't know how long we stood looking up at the sky. Presently the tiny dots became specks and a moment later, blinking my eyes against the strain, I stared again, and they were gone.

For a time I simply held Becky, squeezing her to me. Then I was aware of the murmur again—quieter now, and more subdued—of the voices around us. We looked up, and they were moving, past us and beyond us, on up the hill back to the doomed town they had come from. They straggled by, their faces bland and emotionless, a few of them glancing at us as they passed, most of them not even interested now. Then Becky and I walked down the hill, passing through them—dirty, our clothes smeared and wrinkled, and we limped, shuffling through the grass and weeds, one shoe off, one shoe on, in awkward stumbling victory. Silently we passed the last of the figures around us, and then we were walking down the slope through the weeds toward the freeway and the rest of our kind.

We stayed, that night, with the Belicecs. We found them in their home, where they'd been held, fighting sleep to the end—released now and free. Theodora was asleep in a chair; Jack sat staring out his great front window, waiting for us. There wasn't actually much to be said, though we said it, grinning with weary elation. Then, within twenty minutes, we were each of us lying in exhausted sleep.

It didn't even reach the papers, this particular story. Drive across Golden Gate Bridge into Marin County today, make your way to Mill Valley, and you'll simply see a town, in a few places a little shabbier and run-down than it quite ought to be, but—not startlingly so. The people, some of them, around the bookstore plaza, for example, may seem to you strange, listless and uncommunicative, and may impress you as a little weird. You'll see more houses empty and for sale than can quite be accounted for; the death rate here is rather higher than the county average, and sometimes it's hard to know just what to write down on a death certificate. On and around certain areas clumps of trees, patches of vegetation, and occasional animals sometimes die from no apparent cause.

But all in all, there's nothing much to see in, or say about, Mill Valley. The empty houses are filling quickly—it's a crowded county and state—and there are new people, most of them young and with children, in town. There's a young couple from Nevada living next door to Becky and me, and another—we don't know their name yet—just across the street in the old Greeson place. In a year, maybe two, or three, Mill Valley will seem no different to the eye from any other small town. In five years, perhaps less, it will be no different. And what once happened here will have faded into final unbelievability.

Even now—so soon—there are times, and they come more frequently, when I'm no longer certain in my mind of just what we did see, or of what really happened here. I think it's perfectly possible that we didn't actually see, or correctly interpret, everything that happened, or that we thought had happened. I don't know, I can't say; the human mind exaggerates and deceives itself. And I don't much care; we're together, Becky and I, for better or worse.

But . . . showers of small frogs, tiny fish, and mysterious rains of pebbles sometimes fall from out of the skies. Here and there, with no possible explanation, men are burned to death inside their clothes. And once in a while, the orderly, immutable sequences of time itself are inexplicably shifted and altered. You read these occasional queer little stories, humorously written, tongue-in-cheek, most of the time; or you have vague distorted rumors of them. And this much I know. Some of them—*some* of them—are true.